# Journey to Maidenstone

*Tales of the Skygrass Kingdom*
*Volume I*

## Lynda J. Farquhar

*Cover art by Maeve Pascoe*

I dedicate

# Journey to Maidenstone

To all nine of my Granddaughters

Coryn, Kristyn, Katie, Hannah, Alana,
Mallory, Kayla, Cassidy & Elissa
With hopes this book will encourage them
To search for their own destiny

## Settings

| | |
|---|---|
| Talin | One of Twelve Valleys along the Green River |
| Namché | City at base of Mountains Wool Market |
| Maidenstone | Ancient Lamasery where Sab-ra goes to school |
| Natil | King's Valley, government for all twelve valleys |
| Skygrass | Legendary valley, location of blue diamond mine |
| Halfhigh | Way-station on journey from Talin to Skygrass |

## Names of Major Characters

| | |
|---|---|
| Sab-ra | Healer, Empath and Priestess |
| Ellani | Grandmother to Sab-ra, Midwife |
| Silo'am | Grandfather to Sab-ra, Head of the Silversmith Guild |
| Hent | Uncle to Sab-ra |
| Dani | Father to Sab-ra, died in ice crevasse fall |
| Ashlin | Mother to Sab-ra, wife of Dani, sister to Linc |
| Conquin | Best friend of Sab-ra, aide to Queen Verde, Empath |

## Names of Characters at Maidenstone House

| | |
|---|---|
| Falcon | Mistress of Maidenstone, Priestess and Empath |
| Honus | Cook at Maidenstone House |
| Jun | Empath Teacher, Maidenstone House |
| Marzun | Head Empath, Maidenstone House |
| Ann Mali | Physician, Healer at Maidenstone |
| Te Ran | Head Priestess, Far-Seer |
| Tol Mec | Girl who keeps Cloudheart from cooking pots |
| Gordo | Gemstone merchant |

## Characters from Army & 12<sup>th</sup> Valley

| | |
|---|---|
| Grieg | Captain of Garrison, obsessed with Sab-ra |
| Justyn | Translator falls in love with Sab-ra |
| Ruisenor | King of Twelve Valleys |
| Verde | First Queen of Twelve Valleys |
| Ion'li | First Consort, Second Queen |

## Kosi Warriors & Bearer

| | |
|---|---|
| Say'f | Warrior King of Kosi tribe |
| Ghang | Mercenary Kosi guard at Maidenstone |
| Rohr | Kosi Warrior, assigned to protect Sab-ra |
| Ten-Singh | Bearer guard Member of the Resistance |

## Names of Months in Skygrass Kingdom

| | |
|---|---|
| Moon of Snows | January |
| Hunger Moon | February |
| Vernal Moon | March |
| Waking Moon | April |
| Planting Moon | May |
| Flowering Moon | June |
| Ripening Moon | July |
| Thunder Moon | August |
| Harvest Moon | September |
| Red Leaf Moon | October |
| Black Twig Moon | November |
| Long Night Moon | December |

To Kel & Don,
you always lift
my spirits

Lynn

## Chapter 1 – The Survival Test
## Harvest Moon, 9<sup>th</sup> month

The snows came early that year. By the time of the Harvest Moon, snowdrifts already girded the loins of the Blue Mountains. The barbarous Kosi, black-skinned Warriors who rode the endless grass plains, had recently stepped up their abductions of our fertile young mothers. The People trained their children to spy on the Kosi, reporting on their movements and warning the Elders of an impending attack. However, the Elders permitted no child to spy before successfully completing a Survival Test.

When the Spymaster told us to make ready for our Test, I quivered, knowing Hodi and I would be abandoned in the high range. Using only our skills, we would have to find our way back home to the valley of Talin. Hodi was thirteen, a bright-eyed boy with shiny dark hair. He was my spy partner, my little spirit brother. I was fifteen, gangly like a colt and my red hair and gray eyes made the other spy children look away whenever they saw me. Hodi was my lifeline, the only child who would train with me. Talin's golden wheat fields were our schoolrooms. It was there we learned to locate each other with birdcalls and to send coded messages using white thuringa stones. It was the happiest time of my life.

The Spymaster met us in the stable. It was warm from the bodies of the livestock and filled with the scent of fresh cut hay. We rode out of Talin on our ponies, my Yellowmane and Hodi's Sorrell. The cool blessing of the Wind Goddess caressed my skin and I caught the scent of the pink laelia flower as we descended the mesa.

Once at the base, the Spymaster blindfolded us with strips of soft black wool. All night we rode up the mountain; the Spymaster leading our ponies by their reins.

When we peeled the blindfolds off our eyes the next morning, we saw no food, no waterskins and no map. I found the homeward trail almost by accident on the third day. Seeing it, I felt a rush of warmth race through my body.

Hodi spotted the boot-shaped mesa standing like a stair step against the folded land two days later. The golden wheat fields of Talin had never looked so welcoming. Talin was one of twelve valleys in a kingdom strung along the Green River. Each valley had a role to play, but Talin was the most important because the Guildmasters of Talin guarded a mine of blue Skygrass Stones hidden high in the secret Skygrass Valley.

"It's the last ascent to the village, Sab-ra," Hodi's black eyes sparkled and his dark hair blew wildly. "Not a single child spy ever finished the Survival Test this fast."

"You wouldn't have gotten back at all without me," I yelled, laughing at him over the sound of the running ponies. I raised both my arms in a salute to our success, gripping my pony's flanks with my thighs. The last yellow leaves swirled in the air above us, lifting my red curls. Side by side, we raced the winding road to the top of the mesa and pulled up hard.

I was surprised to see the People already taking their places around the Summoner at the Communal Flame. Sundown was an hour away. All of the old women and many of the men had been weeping. Even the children were unnaturally quiet.

"Grandfather, I'm back," I called, hoping to see pride on his face.

He saw me and scowled. "Stable your mount, Sab-ra. Sit here with your Grandmother."

My throat closed. I slid off Yellowmane and led her to the stable. I handed her reins to Chiyo. He was a fierce boy, an older child spy.

"What happened?" I asked, although I knew—the Warriors had struck again.

"While you were gone, the Kosi took seven women and this time they killed their husbands."

Blood rushed to my core. I put a hand on the stable door to get my balance and made a silent vow. I would not sit by while these barbarians destroyed our race. With every bone in my body, I wanted to save our women from the Kosi.

The Communal Flame in the center of the village was the place where the Elders made important decisions and held significant ceremonies. As Hodi and I walked forward to take our places, my chest tightened as I thought about the recent Kosi attack. When Hodi looked at me, I could tell he struggled with the same whirlwind of emotions. I tried to raise my spirits, remembering that tonight Grandfather would keep his promise from many years ago. Tonight I would receive the fabled necklace of Skygrass Stones.

"Welcome, Sab-ra and Hodi," the Summoner proclaimed. He wore a long ceremonial robe and hit firesticks together above his head to begin the ritual. They shone in the air like fireflies. "The Elders are pleased to see you safely returned from your Survival Test. We celebrate your achievement."

His words were appropriate, but his voice was ragged and far from festive.

Grandfather rose and called me to stand beside him. "Sab-ra, joy of many years, I have a gift for you."

He raised a silver circlet set with magnificent Skygrass Stones over my wild red curls.

"I present you with the most desirable piece of jewelry in the Twelve Valleys. I call it the Stars of Evening."

He placed the band around my throat, fastening its clasp. My breath caught high in my chest. The tribute I had worked so hard to earn was mine. The People applauded. The stone's facets caught the firelight, and I launched myself into Grandfather's strong arms.

He murmured, "Well done, Spy child, well done."

I wanted him to recognize how hard I'd worked. I wanted him to know how much I longed for his approval, but Grandfather pried my arms from his neck and set me firmly on the ground. Looking up at his face, I slowly unclasped the necklace. In the face of the Elders' grief, and Grandfather's obvious despair, I didn't feel I should wear the blue gemstones from our hidden mine in the high range. Hodi's father stood and asked his son to rise. He presented Hodi with a leather sack bulging with Skygrass Stones. He quietly said the incantation that sealed the packs. No outsider could open the container now.

"Your mother's gallant spirit lives in you," he told Hodi, a forced smile on his lips. Hodi glanced at me and I knew how much he missed his mother. He would have given anything for her to see his triumph. The Kosi took her years ago.

"Everyone, please be seated," the Summoner announced. "Sadly, we must turn our minds away from the triumphs of our children to discuss Talin's response to the recent Kosi raid." He took a deep breath. "This marauding must be stopped. Let us hear the People's words."

The young men stood glowering with arms folded across their chests. Others reached for their children. The few young women we had never came outside any more. No one spoke.

In the quiet, the fire snapped and a burning coal rolled toward me. I was that coal of fire. I burned to end this reign of terror.

—

"I hear no rage from the People," Grandfather roared. His voice was full of contempt.

"Shall we gather our few remaining young women and simply *give* them to the barbarians? Is this to be the last generation of the People? Will the guardians of the great Skygrass Stone mine become extinct?"

Taking a deep breath, I stood, pulling Hodi up beside me. I saw startled looks from the men and a scowl from Grandfather.

"Elders of Talin, I wish to tell you my idea for rescuing our women."

"Sab-ra, sit," Grandfather hissed. "You are only a young girl. This is business for the Elders."

"I would hear what she has to say," the Summoner said calmly.

"Hodi and I could carry Lethal Sleep to our captive women. They could drug the Warriors. When the foul beasts lie cold, we will lead the women home."

Lethal Sleep was a purple berry the People used on dying animals to hasten their journey to the skies. Most of the Elders' faces were horrified, but others looked at me with narrowed eyes, respectfully. My People had been pacifists for a thousand years. In the mores of our culture, proposing to kill an enemy was shocking, profane and sacrilegious. The Elders banged their staves on the stone. Grandfather stepped square in front of the Flame.

"Sab-ra, you know nothing of these depraved brutes. The most recent raid bears the marks of the Shunned. They are vicious animals." His tone was strained and cold. The heat of anger flooded my body. With a wave of his hand, he had discarded me.

"We thank you for your bold idea, Sab-ra," the Summoner announced, "but it is time for you to leave us. The Council will make our decision after you and Hodi depart."

We trudged away, discouraged, but once out of sight we ducked behind some low shrubs. The men resumed the debate. The acrimonious words continued for a long time. When the voices finally ceased, the Summoner spoke.

"I have reached my decision. I am the Keeper of the Past, but the time for meditation and prayer has vanished. Lethal Sleep is a drastic idea, but these are dire times. Chiyo found the Kosi Green River camp a few days ago. Now that we know the camp's location, Sab-ra and Hodi will trail the Wool Caravan out of Talin in the morning. They will deliver the poison. They will be the vectors of Talin's revenge."

The Summoner asked those in favor to bang their staves. The sound was thunderous, and the Council slowly dispersed.

"I want revenge on the Kosi who took my mother," Hodi said bitterly. "I would kill him with my bare hands if I could."

"You would keep that pleasure all to yourself?" Amusement turned my lips up. "I will go with you, Hodi. Together we will poison the animal who stole your mother."

## Chapter 2 – The Camp of the Shunned

I woke to the sound of the Wool Drivers harnessing the Ghat, the shaggy horned cattle of the high range the People trained to pull our wool wagons. Each year, during the Harvest Moon, men of Talin undertook the dangerous journey to the base of the great Dhali Ra Mountain to sell our wares in the mystic city of Namché. Dressing hurriedly, I climbed the ladder from my loft down to the kitchen. I wore tasuede pants, a jacket and boots lined in Ghat fur. I grabbed a dark hat to cover my red hair. At the last moment, I decided I would wear my necklace. I placed the stone-studded band around my neck proudly.

I reached out to hug Grandmother, who did not return my warm greeting. I turned my face away, not wanting her to see my disappointment. She handed me a packet of tsampa bread and—tightly sealed in waxy hide—the Lethal Sleep berries. My first mission was commencing. I took a deep breath, strengthening myself for the task. Grandmother whispered the Travelers Blessing over my head.

"You are only carrying a message as you have done a hundred times before," she said, trivializing my fears. Her lack of caring hurt me deeply. My Grandparents took me in after my parents died, but they always treated me as a burden.

Turning to Grandfather, my chest tightened hard. I wanted him to forgive my defiance in front of the Elders the previous night.

"Guildmaster of Talin, may I have your blessing?"

When he hesitated, Grandmother glowered at him. I wondered if she knew how important his blessing was to me or if she was just placating the spirits.

He stood and ripped the necklace from my throat. It hurt so much; no words would come from my open mouth.

"That is for despising your own life, Granddaughter. Now go. And don't die."

As I walked from the house, I heard Grandmother's voice from the open window.

"I thought you made that necklace for your granddaughter."

"I have no granddaughter now, only a young fool who gave her life to the Shunned."

Rage wrapped her dark cloak around me. I would succeed and return, just to show Grandfather how wrong he was.


We parted from the Wool Caravan drivers the morning of the third day. They wished us luck as they turned the wool wagons south to Namché. We travelled east, riding uphill through golden aspens, following Chiyo's map. The tops of the trees bent toward each other, creating a green-gold arch. Late in the day, we glimpsed the Green River shining through the trees. Chiyo told us the Kosi camp was near a bend in the river where the moving waters left a golden crescent of sand.

Like silent dusky deer, we descended to the flat plain across the water from the sandy cover and set up camp. We tied our ponies to trees near a spring and filled our waterskins with icy water. A screen of sentinel pine trees hid our campsite.

"One of us should stay with the ponies," Hodi whispered. "Do you want to scout the camp to see if they have our women?"

My heart beat so rapidly, I could feel pounding in my temples. I dreaded going closer, but because I was two years older, the Elders made me the leader of the mission.

In the silence, his whisper was teasing.

"You are only a little girl. I am stronger. I will go."

"No, Hodi." I grabbed for his hand. "We should go together, shoulder to shoulder as we always have. Don't you remember the first cannon of spy training? I quoted the Spymaster saying, "Facing your enemies, back to back, or shoulder to shoulder…

Hodi finished my sentence "…creates a circle of power and intimidates the enemy."

I forced a smile to hide my apprehensions. My abdomen was lurching like an unbroken Ghat. We nodded at each other, never closer than when we were in danger.


Crouching, we inched through the remnants of the forest, where small trees disappeared into a marsh. Our footsteps sank into the oozy muck and I saw a tiny butterfly, blue as a Skygrass Stone, feeding on salt. When we reached the border of reeds by the water, a flock of dragonflies rose into the air like flying jewels—green, red and yellow—their bodies as long as arrows.

I opened a peephole in the reeds and drew in a sharp breath. Descriptions of the appalling Kosi did not prepare me for their enormity; these men were giants. Fear took me up into her arms. I stood defenseless within a few paces of the enemy.

Two dogs stood near the dark leather flap tents. Their bodies were white, except for tan spots on their hips and backs. They loped toward the perimeter of the camp and raised their muzzles to scent the air. These were the legendary gazehounds. Their enormous eyes could spot game a hundred thent away, in the air or on the ground. I whispered a brief prayer to the Wind Goddess, felt the breeze change direction and knew she blew our scent away. The regal dogs trotted back to the camp.

The Kosi Warriors had copper-colored skin and black hair coiled around their heads. Leather straps stretched diagonally across their bare chests from shoulder to waist. They were practicing with bows and arrows. The arrows thunked as they hit small dead animals tied to trees as targets. Birds of prey stood on the bent arms of two of the Warriors. The raptors' yellow beaks curved sharply. Leather helmets completely covered the eagle's eyes, until their trainers removed the hoods, setting them free to kill. One of the old men in our village swore he'd seen an eagle kill a rock mammal by circling above the gazehound who was waiting near the creature's nest. Screaming through the skies, the eagle swooped down, snatched the prey and carried it to a Kosi Warrior standing on a high peak. The eagle and the gazehound were partners in the hunt—the spy children of the brutal Kosi.

Later, more men thundered in on shining horses. They rode as if merged with their mounts. Dead chanry birds hung from their saddle horns. The men removed the birds' feathers and tied them to a pole across the campfire. The smell of the roasting fowl made Hodi's stomach growl. I smacked him. He ate a piece of tsampa bread to deaden his hunger.

I could hear my heart beat loud as the staves hitting the ground around the Communal Flame. I wanted desperately to succeed, but at that moment, I deplored the impulsiveness that led me to propose this mission. I had no one to blame but myself.

It was dark before we spotted a woman. She was Kosi, copper skinned with a tattooed forehead. Dressed in black, she wore the faces of the moon on silver discs around her throat. She examined the ground carefully, apparently checking for serpents. I glanced at Hodi. His dark eyes were huge with fear.

The Kosi woman opened the flap of the largest tent, and three more women emerged. Two were Kosi; one was from the People. Anxiety leapt up and clutched my throat.

If we had seen no women of the People, we could have returned to the forest—honor intact—and ridden back to Talin.

Now, there was no choice. I reached for Hodi's hand. His fingers trembled, cold in my grasp.

"Is it your Mother?" I whispered.

He shook his head and whispered, "No."

The women walked silently through sandy scrub, following an armed Warrior. They stepped between bushes whose silver leaves reflected the moon's light. The wind molded the dark fabric to the women's strong bodies. Their long gowns brushed against the sand and bare toes showed at each forward step. The river was close by, only a hundred paces from their camp. The moving water tumbled over stones, making the only sound except our rapid breathing.

The Kosi guard stripped a spear from the leather strap across his back and walked downriver. When he turned away, the women pulled dark dresses over their heads and stood in the moonlight, naked. The three Kosi women entered the river. They swam like otters, the phosphorescent water gilding their skin. The moon made a shining road across the river, coaxing them further into the current.

I inched closer, darting from one shadowed rock to another. I could hear Hodi's footsteps and rapid breathing behind me. I closed my eyes in fright, trembling all over. Hodi hit my shoulder and pointed. The ivory-skinned woman from the People was swimming across the river toward the reeds on our side. She emerged from the water and sat in the shallows, washing her skin with soap grass.

"Go back to the ponies," I whispered. "I will give her the Lethal Sleep and tell her the rescue plan." After a long hesitation, Hodi nodded. His face was expressionless. In the gloom, I scurried closer. Reaching the reeds just behind the seated woman, I fell to my knees and slid my hand across her mouth.

She bit down on my hand, trying to twist out of my grasp. My fingers were slick with fear-sweat, and my hand slipped from her face. I grabbed her head, holding her tight against my body. She struggled violently and opened her mouth to bite me again. I shoved the tip of my knife into the back of her neck.

"It is Sab-ra from Talin." I waited and she stopped moving. "These are Lethal Sleep berries from the mountains. Crush them and mix the powder into the waterskins. Make the Kosi Warriors drink the poisoned water on the first night of the Red Leaf Moon. Come to the river with your sisters from the Twelve Valleys. We will be waiting."

"Will the men die?" she whispered.

"Yes," I murmured and crept away, my whole body tingling with pride—I had succeeded. Running bent over, I risked raising my eyes to see if the Kosi guard had returned. I saw him. Slowly he turned his predator gaze in my direction. His countenance was broad and cruel looking. He had one white eye. He took a step toward my hiding place. I fell to the sands, trembling.

A sudden cry rent the air, sounding like a dire wolf pup. The Warrior turned toward the sound taking huge strides away from me. He bent down, fighting with something in the grass. Panic took me, and I bit the inside of my bottom lip to keep from screaming. The Warrior stood up and called the women. Immediately the women left the water, dressed and started back to the camp. The Warrior had tied something to his back. In the dark, I could tell that it was struggling. I prayed he had captured an animal. As soon as they walked away, I stood up and raced deep into the forest.

When at last I found our camp, Hodi was not there. I called his name repeatedly in a harsh whisper. Unable to do anything else in the darkness, I covered myself with furs. Tomorrow I would find him, my little spirit brother. I fell into an exhausted sleep.

# Chapter 3 – Finding Hodi

I woke to dark clouds scudding across the sky. Hodi was still missing. The success of my mission was nothing now. All I wanted was to find my spy partner. The arrangement of our camping gear was unchanged since the evening we left for the river. Hodi had been gone all night. Worry laid her icy hands upon my shoulders.

Grabbing some bread and cheese, I checked on the horses, got them water and began walking east. When the sun told me I had walked for an hour with no sign of Hodi, I returned to the camp. For another two hours, I made larger circles, calling and watching for any movement in the brush. By late afternoon, I knew I had to get closer to the Kosi camp. I had to see if the game animal tied to the Warrior's back was my partner. My breathing shuddered.

I waited until dusk to bring the ponies closer to the river. After tying them securely in a dense wooded area, I crept into the reeds. The Warriors were grooming their horses, and the women were preparing the evening meal. The scent of roasting chanry filled the air. I would wait until Darkness unfurled her cloak before swimming across the river to the camp. There was no choice now, but thinking about getting that close to the barbarians, my heart dove deep within me. My breathing came in short bursts.

When all the Kosi entered their tents and there had been no sound for over two hours, I walked to the steep riverbank, removed my boots and slid suddenly to the bottom. The sound of my feet hitting the water made me gasp.

I glanced at the leather tents, but no one emerged. I lowered my body into the ripping pull of the current. The clay river bottom was slippery, and the mire sucked at my toes.

Taking a deep breath, I ducked underwater and swam.

When I reached the other side, I crawled up the bank feeling sharp spice branches poke into my belly. At the top of the bank, I flattened myself. Raising my head slowly, I saw him.

The wretched Kosi had tied Hodi to a tree. My spy partner had made the dire wolf's cry to draw the Kosi guard's eyes away from me. Desolation made my head ring in pain. His was moving, I told myself. The Kosi hadn't killed him. I could still rescue him.

The camp was silent. Even the campfire was doused. My teeth chattered from cold and fright, but I forced myself to steal through the darkness until I found some dense shrubs near the tents. Panting in fear, I hid in their deepest shadows. Trying to slow my breathing, I called upon the spirit within and made the cry of the dipper bird. Hodi did not answer.

I caught a sudden movement out of the corner of my eye and turned my head. A gazehound stood beside me. Quivering, I made the hand sign telling him to lie down. He lowered his graceful body to the sand. Trying to look confident, I ran quickly to Hodi's tree.

"Hodi," I whispered.

My spy partner raised his head slightly. I caught the metallic smell of blood. A long cut crossed his forehead. The Kosi had peeled his scalp back. In the moonlight, I could see a white piece of bone. The sight was ghastly and bile rose, searing the inside of my throat. I gagged.

Kneeling at his feet to untie his bonds, I felt warm breathing on my back. Looking over my shoulder, I saw the gazehound's eyes.

"Down," I hissed in a fierce whisper, pointing to the sand. He lowered his body. When I had all the knots untied, I whispered, "Hodi, can you hear me?" He moaned. A wave of fear and pain streamed from him.

"You have to try, my partner. If we can make the river, I will float you across. You can ride Sorrell home."

One of Hodi's fingers twitched, but when I lifted him to his feet, he collapsed. He was far heavier than I remembered—dead weight. I maneuvered him behind me and grabbed his arms, positioning them around my neck. Holding his hands together at my throat with one hand, I used the other hand to boost him up on my back. Bent over, I plodded away from the camp. The blood from his wound dripped on my neck. The odor was salty. Extreme nausea nearly made me retch, but I forced myself to go on.

I had taken only a dozen steps when the dog brushed against my side. His back came up to my waist. Fast as the river in spate, he moved in front of me and stood still. I turned to the left. Another dog appeared. Two more emerged from the blackness. The four of them made a tight circle around us.

"Down," I hissed.

The dogs locked eyes with each other. All four of them opened their jaws and made a high moan like a lynx. I swung my body in the direction of the river trying to get past their bodies, but one of the dogs pushed against the backs of my legs, and I went down on my knees. Hodi slid off my back.

"Get up. Run," I whispered at him fiercely. He made no response. I started crawling, dragging Hodi behind me. We reached a downward slope, and I rolled Hodi toward the river. Behind me, a tent flap opened. Terror flared in my belly. Two Kosi Warriors emerged and yelled a command to the dogs. They melted like shadows.

I peered around desperately but couldn't see Hodi in the darkness. Had he made it to the river? The Warriors wrenched me upright. One hit me hard just below my ribs. The blow forced the air from my lungs.

The pain was excruciating. I struggled to breathe, nearly bent in half. They forced my arms behind me and tied them together. One Warrior held me while the white eyed Kosi hit me repeatedly on the face, chest and shoulders.

I screamed for help. He kept pummeling me. I struggled, trying to bite him. I saw the other warriors standing outside their tents—spectators watching a challenge match between a small girl and a large dark animal. A woman emerged, but one of the Kosi shoved her back into the tent.

The Warriors wrenched me to my feet and dragged me to the Hodi tree. They tied me to the rough bark. I screamed in rage. The white eyed Kosi grabbed a piece of leather. He stuck his fingers in my mouth and forced my jaw open. I tried to bite down. He tied the strip across my open mouth and around my head. I gagged, swallowing convulsively. They stood there a few moments, surveying me. One of them went down toward the river but came back without Hodi. Darkness came over me like a hood. My grasp on life lessened. I fought against the pull to give up. I wanted to live; I wanted to rescue Hodi.

Tied up, beaten and in severe pain I could do nothing but wait for dawn. When the sky turned gray, I searched the area with my eyes. Shrubs and scattered large boulders made patchy shadows. I could not tell if the shadows hid Hodi. When the sun rose, I heard an argument coming from the tent. A Kosi woman yelled loudly and stalked outside. She stared at me and then removed my gag. I swallowed repeatedly, trying to lubricate the inside of my mouth with my tongue. When I could speak, I thanked her repeatedly.

She knelt and untied me. I collapsed on the sand. She pulled me up, handed me a flat piece of antl hide with some characters burned into the surface and waved her hands in the air, telling me I could leave.

I took a step but fell again. She yanked me to my feet. I kept trying to gain control of my legs. They wouldn't do what I wanted. I started to cry. The Kosi woman slapped me, the world straightened, and although I stumbled, I reached the edge of the river.

Splashing water on my face and hands, I hunkered down behind a large boulder, hidden from the eyes of the camp. I could glimpse Yellowmane moving through the trees on the other side of the river but could not see Sorrell. A surge of relief slowed my breathing. Hodi must have made it, gotten across and left for Talin.

I edged down the bank and felt the icy cold water hit my feet. The near freezing temperature woke me completely. I sank down shuddering, immersed in the frigid river. I crawled through the muck and sticky clay, feeling fish bodies move against me. When the water got deep enough, I dog paddled.

The crossing seemed to take forever, but I emerged at last, struggled to my feet and stumbled to the tree where I left Sorrell. Someone must have untied her lead because she was gone. I prayed it was Hodi. In case he was hiding nearby, I took five white thuringa stones from my pocket. My clothes were drenched, and I was quaking. The stones were wet and hard to grasp. Shakily, I made a pointed arrow with three stones in a triangle and two as a tail. In case Hodi hadn't already left, the sign told him I had returned to Talin.

Hauling my battered body up onto Yellowmane's back, I lay still, trying to block waves of pain and dizziness. I raised my head to view the Kosi camp.

The four gazehounds stood on the riverbank watching me. Groaning, I bent forward, wrapped my arms around Yellowmane's neck and kicked her lightly in the flanks. She turned toward the forest. I looked back over my shoulder. The gazehounds raised their muzzles in the air and made the moaning feral cry. My spine tingled.

Thus bruised and barely conscious, I began my dejected return to Talin. I would have to face the Elders, to face my failure, to face my punishment.

## Chapter 4 – Returning to Talin

Riding the twisting road up to Talin's plateau, misery slowed my breathing. I feared the Elders' repercussions. I would tell them everything I had done to save my partner. I would make them understand how much I hated leaving with Hodi's fate unknown. I desperately wanted forgiveness.

When I rode up to my house, my Grandparents rushed outside.

"Where is Hodi?" Grandfather asked. He got a shoulder under my right arm and lifted me off Yellowmane. "What happened at the Kosi camp?"

"Isn't he here?" They shook their heads, looking confused. "Can we just go inside? I need to sit for a moment." Riding home had increased the aching in my bones. I was so tired I could hardly talk.

Grandfather supported me into the house and soon Grandmother had the water boiling for tea. The fragrance of the brew relaxed me. All I wanted to do was sleep.

"Sab-ra, tell us what happened," Grandmother ordered in a cold voice. She was Healer to all the People in the Twelve Valleys, but she didn't run for bandages or salves for my injuries. She didn't even ask me how I got hurt.

"Tell us," Grandfather's voice was authoritative.

I closed my eyes, hardly able to deal with their angry questions in my pain and awful fatigue.

"When we reached the Kosi camp," I stared down into my empty teacup. "The Kosi were hunting with eagles and gazehounds. The animals are partners…"

"Sab-ra," Grandfather's voice was tight. "Stop. Where is Hodi?"

There was a long pause. Both my grandparents' faces were shuttered. The silence was intense.

My right eye would not open all the way. I touched my eyelid with my fingertips, wincing from the pain. They don't care at all about me, or they would help me, instead of asking all these questions. My mouth twisted in resentment.

"Go on," Grandfather's voice was harsh. I could see the veins bulge in his forehead.

"Just give me a moment," I took a deep breath and then said, "We waited until the women came to the river to bathe. One woman was from the People. I gave her the Lethal Sleep leaves and told her the rescue plan."

"Where is your partner?" Grandfather banged his fist on the table, rattling the teacups.

"Please, listen. After I gave the woman the poison I returned to our camp, but Hodi wasn't there. I found him alive the next day. The Kosi had tied him to a tree. I untied him, but he wasn't fully conscious. The Warriors beat me, look," I held out my arms, pushing up my sleeves so they could see the darkening bruises.

Neither of my grandparents spoke. In the silence, I could hear the wind outside the house, keening.

"Near dawn, a Kosi woman came, untied me and gave me this," I handed Grandfather the message. My voice was dark with remorse.

"You left Hodi there?" Grandmother's shrill voice raised an octave. "Did you learn nothing in spy training?"

"You never leave your partner," Grandfather shouted at me. "It is one of the High Rules of Talin. I could beat you myself, I am so angry. Get out of my sight. I must go and tell Hodi's father."

"Hodi is no doubt dead," Grandmother was furious.

"I dread telling Hodi's father," Grandfather told me, shaking his head. "The Elders must decide your fate. I can't think of a punishment severe enough."

I choked back a sob, feeling my grandparents' terrible disappointment. I wanted them to know how hard I'd tried to save my partner, but Grandfather cut me off.

"Sab-ra, you and your uncle Hent will return to the Kosi camp tomorrow. We need to know if Hodi is alive. Possibly he is hurt, unable to get back."

"But I am injured," my voice rose in pain. "I need help." The muscles in my neck cramped down so tight, I could hardly turn my head.

Grandmother slapped my face with the back of her hand.

A hot welt rose on my cheek.

"Your injuries are of no importance," her tone was full of disgust. "On this day I regret I ever took you. You are not of my blood."

I fell to my knees and howled in my rage and pain. Their eyes filled with disgust. They shook their heads and left the room.

I was so tired; I could barely move but finally managed to drag myself to the ladder and climb to my loft. Tomorrow, I would be strong enough to return. Hodi had to be there. I had to find him.


The next morning, Uncle Hent and I rode without stopping until we reached the ridge above the Kosi camp. Although I was nearly falling from the saddle, I was able to point out the site from among the sentinel pines and golden aspen. To my horror, the camp simply wasn't there.

"This is the place," I insisted. "They were here. There were many tents, men and women. I don't understand."

"After you found their camp, they must have moved it. Go back to Talin," he ordered, the set of his mouth tight. "I will find out what happened to Hodi, the partner you abandoned."

I waited until Uncle Hent was out of sight and turned Yellowmane down to the river. I tied her to a weeping shrub overhanging the banks. Perhaps my spy partner had escaped and waited for me still.

I wanted desperately to find him, to see his openhearted smile again. Darting behind tall shrubs into the blue shadows of large boulders, I inched closer to the location of the Kosi camp. Seeing no one, I swam across the river and ran quickly to where I'd last seen Hodi.

On the ground, near the place where the gazehounds trapped me, I saw one white thuringa pebble. It was our sign for retreat, for surrender, for disaster. Hodi knew he was dying. He was telling me to search no longer.

I stayed until the sun went down, calling the "rhee dun dun" cry of the dipper bird, the call used by child spies to communicate with their partners. There was no answer. The ominous silence of the place made me face the truth—Hodi was dead. He must have been very close to death when I cut his bonds. My urging him to escape had been the final blow.

Nightfall came, the temperature fell and a heavy mist lay in ragged folds on the ground. I walked to the edge of the river and took my raxor knife from my pack. I removed my pants and sat down on the sand. There were so many bruises on my legs, clear skin was hard to find. Quivering, I carved the symbol for white-eye and the rune for Kosi into my leg. Once the sign was perfect, running red with blood, I drew a huge "X" with my knife across the cuts. I pledged I would see the Kosi punished, tortured and dead. I would have revenge for Hodi.

"Can you ever forgive me, Hodi?" I asked the wild land around me. There was no reply. The finality of Hodi's death left me sunk in tragedy. A mountain of cruel snow seemed to crush my body flat.

The Elders spent a week discussing my punishment, while my apprehension rose to the shrieking point, before they called me to the Communal Flame. I had avoided everyone, keeping to my small bed, trying to control my thoughts as my mind returned obsessively to Hodi's injuries and the smell of his blood dripping on my neck.

The evening of the seventh day, I overheard Grandmother speaking with one of the Elders in the kitchen.

"I'll have Silo'am bring her to the Flame at sundown," she said.

Grandfather called me down from my loft an hour later. I pretended I was sleeping, but he dragged me out of the house. As I walked to the fire, each step led me closer to the Elders whose faces regarded me with scorn. The Summoner raised his white clad arms asking the Goddess to guide them in deciding my sentence.

"Sab-ra, stand."

"My Elders," I bowed. I was quaking inside and my muscles trembled. "I know I failed. Nothing you can do or say will make me feel worse than I already do. Hodi's spirit haunts my dreams. I must try to free his mother, or his essence will never rise to the clouds. I beg you to give me another chance. Could Chiyo go with me as my partner?"

I stood waiting for their response. The night was cold and the wind piercing. I shivered and hugged my body with crossed arms. No Wind Goddess brushed warm breezes across my skin that night.

The Summoner raised his hands, "The Kosi swine murdered Hodi and left his body behind in a food pit," his voice filled with disgust. "We engaged the Bearer people, who returned Hodi's remains. We gave him a sky burial, appropriate to a young Warrior who died *alone* in battle." The Summoner's eyes scorched mine.

"The camp you and Hodi found was not the dwelling place of the Kosi King but a camp of Shunned Warriors. The message said more would die if we approached their camp again."

I stood silent, shaking. My stomach cramped tight.

"I now pronounce your sentence. You will enter the camp of the Kosi King alone. You will never be given another partner." His face darkened with fury. "The Elders are enraged by your audacity in asking."

"May I have permission to scout for the King's camp now?"

I cleared my throat to keep the Elders from hearing tears in my voice.

"No, and we will hear no more requests. Child spies who disobey the High Rules of Talin receive the utmost penalty. After due deliberation, the Council has decided to send you to Maidenstone. As of this night, you have been banned from the People until you bring our rescued women home."

Banned from the People. No, please Goddess, no. Horror pierced every cell in my body. The torment when I realized Hodi was dead flared anew. The Elders pounded their staves. The throbbing intensified my anguish. To Maidenstone, the sound of the word echoed in my head. I knew Maidenstone was a school in the city of Namché. I had heard the proud Novices of Maidenstone turned to begging, if they failed the tests of skill required by the powerful Mistress who ruled there. How could I ever avenge my partner's death in such a far-flung place?

When we returned to the house after the meeting at the Flame, I begged my Grandparents to protest my banishment. I said I didn't want to leave them. I couldn't go to this Maidenstone School. I had made a vow, a pledge to Hodi. I absolutely would not go, I told them. They didn't even answer.

## Chapter 5 – Journey to Maidenstone
## Red Leaf Moon, 10<sup>th</sup> month

Three days later Grandfather, Uncle Hent and I departed for Maidenstone. The Summoner saw only good omens for the trip, although the skies were dark. The Wind Goddess withheld her blessing, and the cold wind twisted mournfully. The air pressed down on the skin around my eyes. Tiny goose bumps rose on my arms and the back of my neck.

Grandfather and Uncle Hent brought our covered wagon out of the stable. A thin rain misted everything. The wagon had tall sides woven with strips of red and black wool. The top was black leather, pierced with small holes. Grandmother put yellow sedge grasses into the bottom of the wagon and covered them with a pashmin wool blanket. I watched until I saw Grandfather and Uncle Hent busy checking the Ghat harnesses. Then I grabbed Yellowmane's reins and made a dash away from the village. Hent raced after me, grabbed me off Yellowmane, carried me back and locked me in the wagon. Darkness closed over my hopes.

By the time Grandfather released me to eat and relieve myself; we had reached the high pass. From there I could see the Blue Mountains, which encircled the whole country of the Twelve Valleys. The Kingdom seemed a necklace of golden jewels strung along the Green River. When I thought about returning to Talin, those jagged peaks became the teeth of a mountain cat, snapped tight.

Every member of the village had stared at me in contempt. I was dead to the community but free from the High Rules of Talin. I would no longer honor the rule banning the taking of human life in revenge. If I could ever find him, I would kill the man I now called the Kosi Wolf without a shred of remorse.

Grandfather bundled me back into the dark wagon, which swayed back and forth. Trapped in its small closed space, claustrophobia made me frantic. I tried to slow my breathing but could not. I panted in desperation. I put my eye to the cracks between the pieces of wool and begged Grandfather to talk to me. As we traversed the blue range, he told me about a creature part bird and part serpent called the Lakt. He painted a picture for me of their huge wings of skin and poisonous talons. Their cries terrified the Ghat and caused them to stampede. If the Ghat fell from the mountain trails into the ravines, the Lakt gorged on their flesh.

When I asked if any other animals lived in this cold place, his words stunned me. Although most people thought they were mythical, he knew wild mooncats, pure white with tufts of hair on their pointed ears, hunted the heights. The People called them Angelions. He said my parents found a young one near the Skygrass Valley and cared for him until he could hunt for himself. I practically stopped breathing, hoping he would continue. His voice was a whisper when he said, "Your mother loved the Angelion with a pure devotion, more deeply than she had ever loved anyone, even my son, Dani. He could call the rain, but your mother could call the mooncat from its lair."

Lulled by the rolling of the wheels, I was almost asleep when I heard Yellowmane scream in pain. My heart banged inside my chest.

"Die, devil Lakt," Grandfather shouted.

I heard running feet, the flap of large wings and the sound of rocks falling from above us on to the trail. The men were beating on something. I banged on the wagon's door, begging for release. Then I heard a wild keening and the thunk of an arrow.

"What happened? Is she all right? Please let me out."

"Stay where you are, Sab-ra," Grandfather's voice demanded.

"The Lakt attacked Yellowmane," I heard Hent yell.

"Let me out," I screamed, beating against the back door of the wagon.

The door swung open. Grandfather was trying to calm Yellowmane. She reared in terror. Deep open slices marred her neck.

"Did the Lakt do this? Did you kill it?" The horrid thing still flapped on the dusty trail. I could see pieces of Yellowmane's hair and skin under its talons. I wanted to stomp the disgusting creature to death.

"We were trying to get the Lakt's claws out of Yellowmane when someone above us in the mountains shot the beast with an arrow. Still the creature clung to your pony. I had to cut it off. I don't think much poison entered Yellowmane's blood."

The stink of the creature was loathsome, like the smell of the dead snakes. The gray skin wings and red head of the demon repulsed me. I drew back, repelled.

Uncle Hent's mouth curled in repugnance at the reek. He picked the carcass up and threw the body from the cliff.

Long before it hit the bottom of the ravine, more Lakt swarmed, tearing chunks from dead flesh—eating one of their own. I couldn't watch any longer. My belly was sick with nausea.

Using my leather waterskin, I poured water over my pony's cuts to wash away any remaining poison. The Kosi arrow left a small blue mark where the shot pierced the Lakt's body and entered her neck. I opened my healer satchel and spread gel across the torn tissue, pushing the flaps of skin together.

"The arrow that killed the Lakt is Kosi," Hent frowned in confusion seeing the distinctive fletching of the arrow. "The Warriors are nearby. We need to leave."

"Why would the Kosi shoot an arrow to save a pony?" Grandfather asked. "The Kosi don't ride ponies."

"I've heard they brand ponies for small children sometimes," Hent said, shrugging his shoulders.

"Get back into the wagon," Grandfather ordered, pointing.

"No. I want to be with my pony."

He insisted, his voice cold. In the darkness, my resentment rose. Talin's rules governed everything from the times for eating and sleeping, to the training of child spies. I had violated one of their precious High Rules. Apparently, that gave Grandfather the right to lock me up like a criminal.

When we reached the foothills, he released me from the stuffy wagon. Waves of hills and dales, like the bodies of sleeping Goddesses undulated below us. I saw one depression filled with rose-colored grasses. They rippled like fabric in a high wind. Below the pink valley, I saw another filled with plants of a silvery color.

I checked Yellowmane's neck. The cuts left by the Lakt were swollen. I pointed them out to Grandfather, who frowned. He took his knife and slashed the sores open so they would drain.

"Stop," I screamed, "You're hurting her." I grabbed for his hand, but he thrust me aside. I fell to the sand by the trail. I rubbed the side of my neck, feeling Yellowmane's pain. I hated him then. She was my pony. He had no right. He released Yellowmane and gave her reins to me. Although I was many hundreds of thent south of Talin, I jumped on her back and darted back up the trail. Hent caught up with me and forced me back in the wagon.

On the last night of our trip, we camped in the area called the Garden of the Gods. We slept beside enormous warm boulders, on a dun-colored plain, in the round black dweli of our ancestors. When the stars came out, Grandfather led me to the edge of the meadow to see my destination. He didn't apologize for cutting Yellowmane. I was still furious. Then, like autumn leaves in a high wind, my angry feelings simply blew away, for far below me lay the fabled city of Namché.

The capital rested on a gigantic mountain with a flat summit. An oval-shaped barrier wall encircled the base of the massive mount. Pale yellow lanterns stood along the lip of the barrier wall sending amber cones of light into the haze.

At the crest of the butte, I saw a structure of colored towers. Six of the towers encircled a seventh taller spire. Arching bridges linked the towers. Swirling fog rose from the foundations, making the bridges look like cranes flying in a huge circle.

Built into the flanks of the mountain, the houses and markets of the city stood on green terraces. Namché shone like a gem wrapped in bridal veil, set in the navel of the Great Mountain Goddess.

"Namché has a different climate than the cold air in the mountains," Grandfather's voice was gruff. "It's always misty there."

"Can we see Maidenstone from here?" I asked. I started to feel better about Grandfather. He had been trying to save Yellowmane's life after all.

"It is those towers," he pointed to the steeples linked by floating bridges.

I was fascinated. The building drew my eyes. I could not look away. A tiny prickle of interest rose inside me. Perhaps I would learn something at Maidenstone, if so it would be something potent. Escape was impossible now, but I would never renounce my vow. The day would come when the Kosi Wolf would die at my hand. Grandfather put his arm around my shoulders and I started to calm down.

"The Lamasery is hundreds of years old," Grandfather said, "Boys study to become monks there, and girls become Empaths, Healers or Priestesses. If a girl chooses to be a Priestess, she accepts being bound to the Temple forever."

"Did the Elders see me staying in the Temple forever?" My voice was high with disbelief.

"Absolutely not," he declared frowning. He took his arm away from my shoulders. "You have a mission to complete. Then you will return, marry and bring children to Talin."

He had never asked about my own dreams for my future. They were irrelevant, it seemed.

That night I dreamed of a guardian spirit, a huge white Angelion with beautiful eyes. She padded silently beside me, her feet leaving blurred footprints in the powdered dust. I wondered if she would be my new partner. Could this giant feline be my guide to the Kosi Wolf?

## Chapter 6 – Entering Namché

Grandfather released me as we approached the outskirts of Namché. He hauled on the reins and brought the Ghat to a stop. As he did so, two massive wooden gates, set deeply into the barrier wall, swung open. The Ghat stomped and quivered; they were close to bolting. Grandfather whipped them repeatedly to make them walk across a triple-arched bridge. Below us swirled a moat full of dark water, smelling of sulphur. Steam rose in tendrils. We were entering a fiercely bubbling cauldron. My fears grew larger than the biggest Ghat.

At the end of the bridge, I saw a vast portcullis gate like the mouth of a leopard with shining metal teeth. When closed, the uppers fit tightly into the pointed lower incisors. Seeking comfort, I held out my hand to Grandfather. He didn't notice. Although he had been to Namché many times, I sensed his uneasiness. The ponies were skittish. We had to force them to advance.

The wagon's wheels ground forward toward the portcullis. Above the snarl of teeth, the leopard's eyes gleamed green. Those eyes scrutinized every person who walked into its jaws. Abruptly the leopard's upper jaw rose in the misty air. The gates screeched—metal on metal—and a Priestess strode out of the mouth through the fog. She carried a lighted candle lantern and seemed more ghost than human.

"Come, Novice," her voice was low but carried clearly across the distance.

I dismounted but would not take a step forward, "I cannot enter the city," I called out. "My pony has been poisoned by the Lakt."

Grandfather shook his head saying, "Sab-ra, go. Hent and I will tend to Yellowmane." I could see exasperation on his face.

---

"Until I know she is safe," I raised my voice fiercely to the Priestess, avoiding Grandfather's angry eyes, "I will not leave her."

The Priestess nodded and walked across the bridge toward us. She slid her hand down Yellowmane's neck and drew a curved knife from her pocket. She voiced an incantation, and Yellowmane stood as if sculpted of stone. The Priestess carved a huge slice of skin from Yellowmane's neck. Beneath her fur, muscles that should have been pink had already turned black. The Priestess cut until she reached clean tissue. I forced myself not to rip her hands away from Yellowmane's neck. My loyal pony endured the horrible pain so bravely. The Priestess peered intently at the small blue indentation from the Kosi arrow.

"It is a bluet mark. A Kosi brand, an evil sign from an evil people." She reached into her robe and took out a tube of silvery white ointment. Shuddering but not attempting to escape, Yellowmane allowed the Priestess to dress the wound in salve.

"I believe she will live."

At the Priestess' words, I sighed in relief. I had been holding my breath since she began her incantation. The Priestess nodded at Grandfather and handed him the tube of ointment.

"Dress the wound each day. The Novice's pony cannot travel until the granulated skin crosses the open wound. The Novice comes with me."

I stood petrified by a whirlwind of feelings. If I entered the city, I would not have the revenge I craved. The swirling world of the Priestess terrified me. I couldn't make myself walk into the Leopard's mouth, which belched out more fog and smoke. I covered my face with my hands, feeling dread on my burning cheeks. The leopard growled, and I wet my pants. Humiliated, I feared the Priestess would know. She held out a hand to me.

"Come along." She looked back over her shoulder at Grandfather saying imperiously, "In two days you may meet with Mistress Falcon."

There was no choice now. The smoke was dense and made my eyes water. I stepped into the Leopard's mouth and entered a dark tunnel filled entirely with smoky fog. The Priestess walked along swiftly, from time to time pulling on my elbow to hurry me forward. Finally, we exited the tunnel. We stood at the bottom of a hundred stair steps. I tilted my head back. I raised my eyes up and then up again. Just as we stepped on the first stair, the mist rose and the air cleared. Suddenly, all of Talin's inviolable rules and punishments flew away like prayer flags in the wind. I heard the mysterious allure of Maidenstone call me, as a mother called her child.

Two days later, I watched from a window in the yellow tower above the stone forecourt of Maidenstone as Grandfather climbed the hundred steps in the pink light of early morning. The mist was rising. The Lamasery seemed to call on the clouds to cloak its beauty. The wind had blown crimson leaves from the trees near the entrance, making skirts of red around their slender gray trunks. When he reached the front door, Grandfather raised his hand and grasped a bell rope.

A silent child opened the door and gestured him into a flagstone-floored entryway. She wore a white dress, and her hair was plaited. She was under a vow of silence, as I had been for days, watched constantly by the black-clad Priestess. She permitted me only to nod or shake my head in response to her questions. I tried to talk at first, but she slapped my mouth every time I said anything.

My Priestess watcher tipped her head to the stairway, indicating I could leave. I walked down the stairs, emerging into the entry. Grandfather reached out and touched my shoulder. Footsteps clicked softly down the corridor. A beautiful raven-haired woman came down the hall. She wore a gown of indigo with a double-stranded White on Ivory Cord around her waist. Grandmother told me anyone who wore the dual stranded Cord had reached the highest strata of the Priestess and Far Reader.

"Silo'am," the woman's voice was resonant, "I am happy to see you here with your granddaughter. She resembles her mother."

I was stunned. How had this woman known my mother? Grandmother told me my mother died at my birth. This woman also knew my Grandfather's name. She did not even use his honorable title but his first name. No one in my village would have dared to do so.

"I greet you, Mistress Falcon," Grandfather lowered his head. "We bring you Sab-ra for schooling at Maidenstone. "My wife, Ellani, has trained her from early childhood to become her successor."

"Since we've had Sab-ra with us, we have learned to our distress she was banned from Talin," her tone was cold.

"True. She violated the highest rule in our culture. She abandoned her spy partner while on a mission. He was scalped and buried in a food pit by the enemy."

"Silo'am, you know well Maidenstone is not for outcastes. We train Empaths, Healers and Priestesses for the Temple. We do not cure disobedience." She turned to me and asked, "Your name is Sab-ra?"

I nodded.

"Good. I see you have learned to hold your tongue. My name is Falcon," she told me, "but you will call me Mistress. Come this way."

The three of us walked down a long hall of windows to a room furnished with a beautifully carved desk. Deeply incised into the Rholam wood I saw hundreds of tiny birds, nests and small branches. Bright woven tapestries hung on the gray rock walls. Mistress gestured to two chairs in front of her desk. We took our seats.

"Guildmaster, I must know more about the circumstances, before I can decide if we will take Sab-ra."

If she wouldn't take me, I worried that Grandfather would bring me back to Talin. If so, the Elders would consign me to the snows.

I had been in the Blue Mountains already with Hodi during our Survival Test. The high range was a death zone. I took a shuddering breath, wondering which future was worse.

"I have thought for many days about this, Mistress. As you know, the People train the children of Talin as spies to inform us when the Kosi intend to make a raid. In living memory, the Kosi had never killed a child. We were appalled when Sab-ra's partner was murdered."

"Go on."

"We did not send Sab-ra to Maidenstone to punish her, despite what she believes. One of the Elders has seen her as a Priestess."

No one ever told me this. I made a strangled noise. Mistress ignored me.

"Since I have your apology, she may stay. However, I need you to know I am agreeing to take her on sufferance, partly because Maidenstone is struggling. We get fewer and fewer novices these days. If Sab-ra succeeds, perhaps more girls will come from the Twelve Valleys."

"Talin wishes to express its gratitude," Grandfather drew a leather pouch from his pocket and spilled a dozen brilliant Skygrass Stones across her desk.

Mistress nodded, acknowledging the gift. "Beyond training Sab-ra further in the healing arts, what do you want her to learn?"

"The Kosi language, if possible," Grandfather's voice was firm. "At some point in the future, Sab-ra must enter the camp of the Kosi King. She needs to be able to communicate with him."

He seemed to have no doubt I would undertake this doomed mission. I blocked the awful picture from my mind, feeling my belly cramp.

"Sab-ra will complete our Empath training first."

"I know little about this Empath training," Grandfather frowned, sounding dubious, "but she is not destined for the Temple."
He tilted his gray head at Mistress, looking determined.

"The Kosi language is very difficult, especially the accent. If she is less than fluent, she will need to understand the enemy without words. Empath training will allow her to read the minds of the Kosi and sense peril before danger strikes."

Amazement pierced me. A thrill ran through my body. I had made the right decision the night I crossed the misty bridge into the leopard's mouth. I wanted this Empath training avidly. Mind reading would help me take my revenge.

Grandfather made a grunting sound. "How long will this take?"

"It depends on Sab-ra's level of diligence and hard work. After she demonstrates mastery of the Empath skills, Sab-ra will take training in midwifery. The Kosi will permit any Midwife into their closed society. Then, we will teach her the Kosi language."

I saw my life stretching out forever in this place. I had just turned sixteen, old enough to be married. I could have screamed in frustration. As Mistress Falcon and Grandfather continued to talk about my preparation, I wandered up the mountain in my mind. I was already homesick. I missed Yellowmane. I even missed Grandmother, although I knew she wouldn't miss me.

Grandfather gathered his things and startled me by taking me into his arms. He had been so gravely disappointed; I didn't think he would ever hug me again. His embrace was a gesture of forgiveness.

"Here is your necklace." I reached out excitedly, but for a moment, he kept it back.

"Promise me to keep the Stars of Evening with you always." His voice was low, his eyes intense and serious.

I nodded. He handed me the beautiful blue diamond necklace. The old man walked down the stone corridor, leaving me a prisoner in this mysterious place.

"Keep Yellowmane safe," I called to his retreating back, feeling the mist of tears, but he didn't respond.

I would keep my vengeance goal alive but knew the time for action lay in the future. The only thing I planned that day was to locate the kitchen and steal a knife. On the day Revenge opened the Leopard Gate, I would be ready.

I began to search for the kitchen. It didn't take long to find it. I hid in the hallway just outside the cooking area, watching two cooks preparing food. One of them was chopping up turnips. When she turned her back to me, I crept forward, grabbed her knife and ran from the room.

I was looking over my shoulder to see if the cooks had noticed and careened right into Mistress Falcon. She stood still, looking down on me and pulled the knife from my hand.

"Why do you need this?" she asked.

I didn't answer.

"We don't allow thieves to become Novices at Maidenstone." She walked past me and returned the knife to the cooks. I stood in the hall waiting, knowing she would punish me.

"You obviously resent being here. You plan to leave at your first opportunity and on your first day, you steal a knife. This is not a good beginning, Sab-ra of Talin."

I waited, feeling sulky and petulant. Sweat beads broke out on my forehead.

"You aren't leaving Maidenstone until I say you may leave. In case you think you can slink through the Leopard Gate without detection, I have informed the guards. If you get that far, they would not let you cross the arched bridge."

I felt a tightening in my chest.

"I have decided to put you in solitary confinement in the morning," Mistress told me calmly.

Late that night I returned to the kitchen and stole another knife.

## Chapter 7 – Solitary Confinement

The masked Priestess took me across the highest bridge into the white tower the following morning. The bridge had no handrails. When I got closer, I looked down and saw that each stair was made of clear glass. They seemed to float in the air. I was terrified, but she turned back and ordered me to follow her. Her face was cold and insistent. I set one foot on the first step. It disappeared in the mist. I raised my eyes to the skies. Step by tentative step, I followed the Priestess.

When we reached the other end of the bridge, she opened a door, gestured for me to enter and told me to wait. I stood just inside the doorway, watching her black robe blow wildly as she returned swiftly to the yellow tower. Looking down the hall behind me, I saw a red robed monk walking toward me. He was old, wrinkled and the top of his head was bald. He smiled gently.

"Come," he beckoned and walked me down the hall toward a small door. He used his key, opened the door and gestured for me to walk inside.

"Why did you bring me here?" I asked.

"Mistress said you were to live here for a while. The cell is not a punishment, Child. Alone, you will learn to concentrate your mind." The monk closed the fitted cubicle door gently, blocking my way out into the corridor.

"No," I screamed, but the door sealed silently. My body grew numb. I wondered if I would pass out. The only light in the room came from a round window in the ceiling, the size of a dinner plate. Inside my prison, I had a hard bed and an animal-skin blanket, nothing else.

Desolation ruled my spirit. The Elders of Talin, my Grandparents and now Mistress Falcon seemed to delight in punishing me.

My mouth clamped tight on the dark taste of bitterness.

I felt the knife that lay in my sash, amazed Mistress had not detected its presence. The monk said the cell was not a punishment, but I knew better.

For many days, I slept, ate and dreamed in the cell. I tried keeping track of time, marking each day with a piece of charcoal I found on the floor. A tray of cold food and water came through a slit in the wall three times a day. When I heard the food bringer approach, I called out asking how long I would be there. The cell door opened. A Priestess dressed in a black dhoti stood in the doorway. She put one finger across her mouth, making the sign for silence.

When she locked the door again, I seemed to see the shadow of an enormous black Lakt watching from the corridor. I knew instantly it was the symbol of my helplessness, my despondency, my despair.

I didn't notice the rat until I woke one night to feel claws on my back. Horror-struck, I flailed at the thing. Its claws scraped on the stone floor, and I shuddered. When the rat got hungry enough, his food would be my fingers and toes. We despise rats in my culture, since they eat the wheat and despoil the wool we sell. Although the cold food that came through the slit was hardly enough for me, I knew I would have to share my meals with the loathsome creature.

Each day, fighting a battle between my own hunger and revulsion, I put some of my food in one corner of the cell. After some time watching the creature, I came to the unwelcome realization the beast was intelligent. He knew when the tray of food was coming, often before I did. He squished himself down on the floor by the food slot, intent on capturing any scraps that fell from the tray. When I scraped his dinner into the corner, his black eyes glittered.

The icy cold forced me to tolerate the rat's warmth in bed. In time, I gave him a name—Melcheese. I called him when his food was ready, and like a trained dog, he ran to his corner.

He enjoyed me scratching him behind his ears.

Sometimes he would roll on his back for me to rub his full belly. Caring for the rat lifted my mood, but only slightly.

The cell grew colder still. The days merged into nights. I tried to raise my spirits by telling myself Mistress would release me in time, but the time kept vanishing. I lived through the days, one moment at a time, but the nights were endless. The walls of the cell closed in.

I recalled the tiny window in the ceiling. By standing my bed on end and climbing up on the headboard, I could just reach the wire grate below the window glass. I ripped off the mesh, cutting my hands. The cuts stung and blood dripped from my fingers, but light poured down into the room. I wrenched the bed apart. Using one of its legs, I banged and struck repeatedly at the glass. Pointed shards fell on my bed. Melcheese shrieked and hid in his corner. The air, the bright cold air, was like a feast.

By re-positioning the bed and jumping up repeatedly, I was able to grip the edge of the window. Tiny triangles of glass cut into my hands. I didn't care. Wrenching my upper body through the tight opening, glass sliced into my breasts, but I was almost out. I forced myself the rest of the way through the open window and stood on the glistening slate rooftops of Maidenstone. I drew the lovely cold air into my body in huge gulps. I had done it. I was free.

Once I removed the shattered triangles of glass from the frame, I could return to my room and escape again without more lacerations. Whenever I came back inside, Melcheese squeaked, happy to see me. He and I were co-conspirators, planning my next foray across the shining slate tiles of Maidenstone's roof.

---

When ice crystals rode the hair of the Wind Goddess, freedom departed. Some days I still conquered the rooftops, but often the cold forced me back into the cell. With the window broken, the cell was almost as cold as the roof. I entered a forest of snow-laden despair.

One morning, Melcheese's scream brought me running back across the slippery slates, covered now in the thinnest coating of ice.

I peered down through the window to see a large black snake strike at him. I pounded on the roof and screamed at it. I had to save Melcheese. I lowered myself down inside. The huge reptile, its yellow eyes flashing had Melcheese cornered. The snake raised its muscular body in the air, hissing. I grabbed Melcheese just before the viper struck.

Holding him in my arms, I backed rapidly away from the snake. We couldn't stay in the cell. While Melcheese and I slept, the disgusting reptile would slay my pet or poison me with its horrible viper bite.

I pushed Melcheese up through the hole and onto the roof. By taking multiple cautious trips, never taking my eyes from the snake, I brought my mattress and blanket to our new kingdom above the snake pit. Now Melcheese and I lived on the icy crown of the world. The viper lay coiled on the remnants of my bed.

We found a part of the roof where the heat vented outside. Protected from the worst of the winds, we made our camp there. Melcheese woke me whenever the Priestess delivered food. By dashing over to the window and leaning down into the cell, I was able to grab the tray before the food splattered to the floor, sustenance for the viper. The loathsome scraping of serpent scales on stones made the hair rise on the back of my neck. I wondered if I jumped down to on of the bridges, whether I could land safely with Melcheese in my arms.

I had been in the cell for about a week when Mistress Falcon stuck her head up through the window calling, "Sab-ra, come down here. Follow me to my office."

I stumbled from the roof down into the cell, my legs wobbly from running on the slanted rooftops. I carried Melcheese snuggled into the crook of my arm.

Mistress led me across the bridge and down many flights of stairs to her beautifully appointed office.

I had been in the darkness for so long, the colors in the hangings glowed like gemstones. Everything seemed too bright. I craved the color like water, desperately.

"I see you have made a friend," her voice was rueful, "And that you escaped the cell." She raised her eyebrows and eyed me intently. "This escape was not what we intended. We intended to have you learn how to conquer loneliness."

I said nothing.

"However, each of us finds her own way to serenity. Yours seems to be in the company of animals. The first step in your training is now complete. Before you begin working with your instructors, I need to tell you what will happen if you disobey them. You are here upon our sufferance. Do you know what the word means, Sab-ra?"

I shook my head.

"It means you will do whatever your teachers tell you to do. If you don't, I will discharge you from Maidenstone. Our rules here are not like the rules in Talin. Their rules preserve a way of life dictated by the Elders. Ours are to help you focus on what you are learning. Let me have the rat. I will take him down to the kitchen."

"His name is Melcheese," I said, handing him to her reluctantly. "Would you please ask the cooks to feed him?"

She tilted her head to the side, looking dubious about my request.

"Please, Mistress, he saved me in the cell."

"I will ask," she paused and settled Melcheese in a drawer in her desk. "Now, while you are here, you will have three instructors. Brother Jun will teach you mind-reading skills, Ann Mali will teach you to be a Healer and Te Ran will teach you the role of the Priestess and Far-Seer. You will begin formal Empath work tomorrow."

The training to let me hear a person's thoughts was beginning. My mind opened wide to receive this wondrous gift. I wanted this skill urgently.

We left Mistress Falcon's office and walked up a flight of stairs and down a hall. I counted the entrances until we reached a wooden door with a rounded top.

When Mistress turned a key and opened the room, I saw two narrow beds with white pillows, blue wool coverlets and a window, a blessed window to the sun. The room was the most beautiful space I had ever seen. Clean white loveliness. My breathing slowed. The room was at least three times the size of my tiny loft in Talin. On one wall, there was a painting of a mountain lake ringed with scarlet fireweed. Could Mistress intend for me to live here by myself?

"No," Mistress said, although I hadn't said anything, "You will share this room with Conquin."

I was bitterly disappointed. I needed time to vanquish the memories of the viper, the cold slippery rooftops, the loss of Hodi and the family I never had. I took several shuddering breaths, trying to gain composure. At least I was out of the cell. As soon as I learned the mind-reading trick, I would leave Maidenstone far behind. I felt the knife that still lay in my sash and smiled in dark satisfaction.

## Chapter 8 – Empath Training

When Conquin herself rushed into the room a few hours later for the first time in many weeks, I felt the soft caress of the Wind Goddess.

"I am Conquin," she announced happily. She had long dark hair in a single braid down her back and a blue crescent moon tattooed above her left eyebrow. I had always wanted to look like her.

"What is your name? What valley do you come from?" Conquin's words tumbled happily from her mouth.

"I am Sab-ra of Talin." I knew I sounded grumpy. I couldn't tear my eyes away from Conquin's pleasure at being here. She smiled at the beautiful view and leaned down to feel the soft beds. Life itself seemed a gift to her.

"I come from Royenal, that's the eleventh valley," she told me. "My grandparents were originally salt sellers. My father devised a way to create the purest white salt from the brown particles gathered on the high ridges. He supplies salt to the King's table. In appreciation, the King himself sent me to Maidenstone."

The girl practically preened herself in delight. She was downright smug. I was going to have to share my room with the recipient of a royal blessing. I flinched from the stark differences between us. A deep thrust of envy racked me, and my heart slowed down so far I felt a hesitation between beats.

Conquin's joy was such a part of her; I doubted she had ever drawn an unloved breath. Why couldn't my life have been like Conquin's? I wanted to have her family and feel the pleasure she found at Maidenstone.

---

"What does your family do in Talin, Sab-ra? How many brothers and sisters do you have? What will you study here?"

Conquin's questions seemed to come in twos or threes. Her words were a ripple of curiosity.

"My parents are dead," I told her.

Sadness creased Conquin's face. She waited for me to continue.

"I live with my grandparents. I am an only child."

"Me too," she responded happily. "I'm taking the Empath training with you. I know we will become best friends."

If Conquin knew anything about my revenge quest, I doubted she would want me for a friend. Still, her enthusiasm was impossible to deny. Despite myself, my spirits lightened.

When her training was complete, Conquin told me she would return to the King's valley to serve Queen Verde herself. I visualized her, seeing a beautiful woman in a lovely white gown. I saw her getting married, holding a smiling baby in her arms and presenting flowers to the Queen, as I thrust a knife into the neck of the Kosi Wolf. We were mountain ranges apart. I had given a vow to tell no one of my mission, so Conquin never knew what my future held; or my plan to escape Maidenstone.


After a breakfast so delicious I could not stop gorging myself, Mistress Falcon took Conquin and me across the hanging bridge leading to the turquoise tower.

My fears rose and rose again as we crossed glass steps above an enormous chasm of air. From the highest arched crescent, I could see the Wool Road curving back up the mountain.

"Aren't you excited, Sab-ra?" Conquin whispered.

"More terrified than excited," I told her quietly.

"I'm not. I'm thrilled to be here. Why would you be frightened?"

I didn't respond, thinking Conquin would probably use her mind reading skills to help little lost children find their mothers. I had a very different purpose in mind.

"You are fortunate to have Brother Jun as a teacher," Mistress told us. "He is extremely skilled. He was the third son of a poor pig farmer. I went to his village to get him when his parents decided to give him to the Lamasery. He was only six years old and very frightened. On our way back to Maidenstone, we came upon a man lying in a ditch. Although he was old and drunk, Jun helped him stand up and gave him what little money his parents sent with him.

"My mood was as black as the pig farmer's fields the day I went to get Jun and he sensed it, young as he was. He took my hand and showed me a beautiful butterfly and later a red-capped kinglet bird. Even feeling the anguish of leaving his family, he reached out to raise my spirits. Jun's soul is filled with compassion."

As she talked about Brother Jun, I noticed Conquin slipping her little hand into Mistress Falcon's. I was stunned. The powerful Mistress of Maidenstone with her absolute authority terrified me. I was so tense my muscles ached. If I had reached for her hand, she probably would have slapped me.

When we reached a door at the end of the bridge, Mistress took a ring of keys from her pocket. The keys clinked. She opened the door and bowed. Tall and slender with dark eyes and a gentle gaze, we saw our teacher waiting. He wore the flowing orange robe of an apprentice monk.

"I am Jun," he smiled at us gently. "I am your Empath teacher."

Jun said we would spend many weeks with him learning to unlock the gates and walk the roads in the minds of others. He would teach us to bring feelings, words or images from a person's mind using only direct thought reading or touch.

He took us to a room filled with wooden niches. Each held a parchment scroll. Jun withdrew one from its case, and the scent of sandalwood rose in the air, so tangible it seemed solid.

Jun carefully unrolled the ancient parchment and asked Conquin to read him a passage. My heart plunged into my belly. How would I ever succeed in learning this? I didn't even know how to read.

Jun took me aside at the end of our session. "Just walk with me. One day at a time." His eyes were kind as he gently touched my shoulder.


Each day Jun sent us into the realm of waking dreams by chanting a calm musical sound. Once we were deep in the trance state, he spoke a single word aloud. When he woke us from trance, he asked for the word.

Day after day, Conquin knew the word. Day after day, I did not. Her skill was infuriating.

After a week, Jun said he would no longer speak the word he wanted us to hear aloud. Instead, he would hold a silent word in his mind, concentrating on it. No word spoke in my mind. Conquin heard the word "moon" on the third day. Jun nodded, looking pleased. I almost hated her then. How did she do it? I was exasperated with myself and felt locked out. It was like being back in Talin where everyone belonged, except me. Tears came into my eyes. I rubbed them away before Conquin of Jun could see them.

"Once you learn this, you will be better than I am," Conquin promised when we crossed the turquoise bridge, returning to our room at evening. I had no such certainties. I was furious with myself. Achieving all my goals depended on learning this skill.

Weeks later, I finally quashed my pride and asked Jun for help.

"I am not hearing your words," I muttered, looking down at the floor, ashamed of my failures.

He gazed at me kindly and touched my forehead. "Because you were able to ask for help, tonight you will walk through fire. Be brave, Sab-ra. Tomorrow, you open the gates of my mind."

That night, as Jun promised, I dreamed I walked between two walls of flame. I strode the path fearlessly, barefoot. Even when sparks hissed on the ground ahead of me or the fire blazed higher, I never hesitated. I was the fire. No firestorm could burn me.

In the morning, I asked Conquin to think of a word. I hoped the fire dream had burned away the locked gateway in her mind, but I couldn't hear a thing.

Depression came down on me like a black wall. I had failed at everything. I had lost Hodi. Grandfather had forced me to come to Maidenstone against my wishes. I didn't know how to read. I couldn't hear a single silent word in Jun's mind. The list of my failures stood stacked atop each other, higher than the Blue Mountains. I could hardly draw a breath.

When we reached the teaching room, Jun read us a passage from one of the scrolls. The smell of sandalwood brought back the first day of Empath training when I found out Conquin could read.

"Wait until you hear a whole sentence," Jun said, looking at me, "Before you tell me what you heard." His confidence almost made me weep.

---

"Cool air rides the autumn leaves," Jun's low musical voice chanted in silence.

The air moved. A glass door slid open in my mind. I heard his words so clearly I thought he had spoken them aloud.

Conquin hesitated. Then in her gentle voice said, "Cool air runs…no. That's not right." Confusion registered in her frown.

"Wait until you hear the rest, and then Sab-ra, I'd like you to recite today," he nodded at me.

"Cool air rides the autumn leaves,

Cloud ponies race mid golden sheaves,

They sing a song,

Of summer's end."


"It's a poem." I said delightedly and quoted the words perfectly. A shiver of pleasure ran down my arms, and Jun drew a round circle blessing in the air above my head.

As we were leaving, Jun told Conquin he needed to talk with me alone for a few minutes. When he closed the door, he turned to me.

"Tell me why you dream of the death of a Kosi Warrior?"

My breathing came quickly. I thought I had blocked the Kosi Wolf from my thoughts during our sessions, but he had easily detected my paltry stratagem.

"Jun, the Kosi Wolf killed my spy partner, Hodi. They put his body in a garbage pit. He does not deserve to live." I felt an intense pain behind my eyes.

"I feel the pain of Hodi's death with you, Sab-ra, but I will not teach a Novice who intends to use her skills to kill," his voice was dark and serious. "I will continue to work with Conquin, but until you can relinquish this quest for revenge, you will work with Ann Mali. Perhaps she can teach you that all of life is precious."

I turned away, burning with embarrassment. I opened the door to leave.

"Wait a moment," Jun touched my arm. "Isn't there something you wanted to give me?"

I looked at him in confusion.

"Sab-ra, the knife," he said, holding out his hand.

I pulled it from my sash and gave it to him, tears of frustration welling from my eyes.

## Chapter 9 - Midwife Training
## Black Twig Moon, 11<sup>th</sup> month

When I entered the Infirmary the following morning, the Healer a woman named Ann Mali, smiled gently at me. Her soft gray curls made tendrils around her face. She was a pudgy woman with white hair and gray eyes. She wore a blue gown as Mistress Falcon did, but hers was bound with the Vermillion Cord of the Healer.

"Welcome, Sab-ra. Have a look around and familiarize yourself with the Infirmary," Ann Mali said. "When you have memorized the layout and the medicines, come over here." She was sitting at a small desk, writing notes.

I looked carefully around the room where Novices came when they needed medical treatment. I knew very ill citizens from Namché also came to the Clinic occasionally. There were six beds, each covered with white linen. A dark blue coverlet lay folded at each bed's foot. At the far end of the room, there was a pine table laden with dozens of small pots sealed with wax, hundreds of stoppered vials and jars of dried herbs. Ann Mali had incised a hangman's noose on the leather pouches containing poisons. Some jars had paper labels with careful drawings of the plants. I recognized sweetsleep, nightshade, wolfsbane and virgin's bower. When I finished my observations, I walked over to Ann Mali's desk and stood beside her desk.

"Please sit here," Ann Mali pointed to a chair. "I am happy to have you as an apprentice, Sab-ra. I was an acolyte at the House of Maidenstone with your Grandmother, Ellani. We took our training as midwives together."

The corners of my lips turned up in a smile. I was immensely cheered to learn she knew Grandmother. Despite Grandmother's resentment of me, she and Grandfather were my only family.

"Please tell me what Grandmother was like when you were students, would you?" I wanted to hear her stories. Perhaps they would help me understand my Grandmother.

"She was much like Mistress describes you—impetuous, determined and quick. She was the best of us at finding herbs growing in the mountains. There were times when I would have given anything to have her abilities."

I sympathized. Her feelings for Grandmother mirrored mine for Conquin.

"When she left here," Ann Mali continued, "she served as an itinerant Healer travelling from valley to valley. Then she met a young man who fell in love with her."

"It must have been my Grandfather. They have been married for many years, and have two sons. The first was my father. I am told he was a beautiful baby."

Ann Mali frowned. "I regret you did not know this before now. The child was not her son but her fosterling. She could not have children."

"That just can't be," I said, confused.

"It is true, Sab-ra. She could not have children of her own."

"What does fosterling mean?"

"Your father was born to one of your Grandmother's patients who died bringing him into the world. Your Grandmother could not forgive herself for the woman's death. She offered to raise the baby, as a penance for the lost mother's life."

My face reddened. Why had my grandparents never shared this with me? Suddenly, Grandmother's words came back to me in a rush, the words she spoke the day I returned to Talin after the abortive mission to the Kosi.

Her words, 'You are not of my blood,' echoed in my head.

Whose blood raced my veins?

Was nothing they told me true? My stomach tightened, and I clenched my fists, my fingernails digging into my palms. My mother, too, had died giving me life. Grandmother said my mother died when I was born, so I could not possibly have remembered her. Yet sometimes when I smelled the perfume of the laelia flower, I seemed to sense her presence.

"Did you know my mother?"

"Yes. I will never forget her wild red curls," Ann Mali smiled at the memory. "She came here before you were born."

Both my mother and Grandmother had been at Maidenstone. Why had my mother come to Namché? Did she come here to train? I had a million questions.

"Could you tell me my mother's name?"

Ann Mali shook her head and took a deep breath. "I'm sorry, Sabra, but Mistress Falcon asked me not to talk about your mother. I have already said too much."

My muscles tensed with bright anger. How dared all these adults keep such secrets from me? I had a right to know my own history.

"Healer training has two parts," Ann Mali said. "The first concerns the identification and drying of medicinal herbs. After you have learned this, we will start seeing patients. We will start today with goldenseal."

Remembering Mistress Falcon saying Midwife training would open the door to the Kosi society, I decided I would learn as much as I could. Perhaps in the Infirmary, I would find a poison to use on the Kosi Wolf.

Ann Mali taught me how to dry plants to preserve their potency and the recipes for potions. She told me we would gather the small clear pearls of the poppy sap when spring came. The milk of the poppy took away pain but Ann Mali called the drug a "Cruel Mistress." If a person took too much, the poppy laughed and took their soul, she told me.

The Black Twig Moon began before Ann Mali said I was ready to go to Namché with her. Learning about herbal medicines had been so easy; I was excited to begin caring for patients. I was determined to succeed, to show Grandmother I was worthy to take over her role as Head Midwife in the Twelve Valleys.

"What are you doing this morning?" I asked Conquin, when we were getting dressed for breakfast. I was so delighted to be going down into the city; I could hardly stop myself from dancing.

"Well, I don't get to go to Namché," Conquin pouted. Then she smiled and took my hands, "I am happy you get to go."

I left for the Infirmary, knowing well all the turns, staircases and most of the bridges leading from the yellow tower to the orange and red spires of the great house. Ann Mali was waiting for me just outside the door to the clinic with her leather medicine satchel. She buckled the satchel on my back. We walked down the hundred steps to the base of the mount.

Gem merchants and silver dealers had their homes high on the mesa. Lower down, the homes were simpler. At the bottom stood the Wool Markets, the shops, the Tea House and the animal auction barns. The poorest people lived beyond the curtain wall. I gave a brief thought to making an escape, but it was winter and without food and a mount, my chances of survival would be nonexistent.

"What patients will we see today?" I asked, happy to feel the cool wind on my skin.

"We will see a young boy bitten by a dog. Later we will see a pregnant woman."

She was treating me like a midwife I realized, and I shivered all over. Soon, I would see the birth of a child, the very beginning of life.

Pleasure washed my face.

In time, I knew I would stand before Mistress and Ann Mali while they tied the Vermillion Cord of the Healer around my waist.

We entered the small wattle house of a young boy. His name was Phin, and he felt very warm when I touched his forehead.

"Will he live, Mistress Mali?" his mother asked Ann Mali. She didn't respond immediately, busy examining the little boy.

"Yes, he will, Mother," I interjected, feeling confident even on my first day as a Healer. Ann Mali's mouth tightened and I had the first inkling this part of my training might not be so easy. We made a tisane for Phin. His mother boiled the liquid over their fire. When the medicine was hot, we took linen cloths and waved the vapor over him. We waited by his bed. Much later, he breathed more easily.

"Did Phin throw a rock at the dog that bit him?" Ann Mali asked.

His mother nodded.

"You must prevent him from ever doing such a thing again. The dog knows him now and will always be afraid. If a dog cringes at your approach, the animal probably carries disease."

"I will make sure, Mistress," the Mother hung her head.

When we left their house, Ann Mali turned to me. Rage crossed her features. "You are not permitted to answer questions from patients. You told Phin's mother her son would live."

"I knew he would live and you didn't answer her when she asked. She needed reassurance." A quick flare of anger took me. Ann Mali was so quick to criticize me, but I was right.

"Right or wrong, you are not ready to respond to patient questions, Sab-ra. You must demonstrate your willingness to learn. You are just a beginner. I am the Healer here. You are only an apprentice."

The black Lakt in my mind watched me with their yellow slit pupils, enjoying my failure.

"I apologize," I said, but heard petulance in my voice.

"There is no need for apology, especially one so insincere," Ann Mali's voice was dry. "However, you will not speak to a patient again until I say you are ready. And if you ever give a patient a prognosis like you did today, you better be right."

I took a deep breath. I thought Ann Mali would be like Jun, kind and helpful. Even Mistress Falcon smiled sweetly at me when I confessed I could not read. Clearly, Ann Mali was more like Grandmother. If I wanted to become a Healer, I would have to dampen my pride and learn what she had to teach me.

"You will return to making tinctures for several more weeks in the Infirmary. During those days, I want you to think about your impetuousness and lack of control."

---

Two long weeks later, Ann Mali told me I could see patients with her again. "I hope you have learned something about yourself during this time, Sab-ra. We are going to visit Hasha and her family this morning. They have four daughters. She is pregnant for her fifth child."

I flushed, embarrassed again about my failure. I was determined to be a perfect apprentice. We walked down the steps to the area of the merchants' houses. The morning was bitterly cold; our breath made white clouds in the air. Ann Mali knocked on the door and our patient, Hasha, invited us inside. She was a plump woman, round and pink as an over-ripe apricot. I could tell from the size of the house and its furnishings that she and her husband were prosperous. Hasha led us back into her kitchen. She bustled around, making tea and humming cheerfully.

"I see we have an acolyte today, Mistress. Tell me your name, Novice."

"I am Sab-ra of Talin." My voice was quiet. I felt sweat on my forehead. I was afraid I would say something wrong.

"Sab-ra is such a lovely name."

"Thank you," I murmured.

She turned to Ann Mali asking, "Mistress Healer, will I have a boy this time?"

"Now Hasha," Ann Mali answered in a chiding tone, "You must trust the gods. Don't you pray for a son?"

"Yes, I pray each night, but so far I have four lovely daughters."

"I must examine you to see if you are progressing properly," Ann Mali's voice was cool and composed. Hasha led the way to her bedroom, and Ann Mali listened to her heart, smelled her breath and felt her belly. "You will deliver soon," Ann Mali sounded pleased.

"I know you can tell whether this one is a boy," Hasha chuckled. "Tell me, and I will give you a golden tsk and ten silver parthats for Maidenstone."

Ann Mali shook her head.

"Then perhaps I will ask the acolyte. Is this the son my husband longs for?"

"I am not far enough along in my training, Mother Hasha," I told her. "I don't answer questions from patients."

"Actually, I believe I will permit the acolyte to answer this question," Ann Mali's face told me this was a test.

"I believe you carry the son you have waited for," my voice was small and thin. I wasn't positive. When Ann Mali nodded, relief flooded my whole body.

Hasha's four small daughters joined us and hugged their large mother. Misery gripped my body. Why had life not given me a mother who loved me as Hasha loved her daughters? I turned away to hide my tears of disappointment. I scrubbed my cheeks with my sleeve. Hasha handed Ann Mali several coins and thanked her for her service.

As we prepared to leave, a sudden quivering deep inside my belly startled me. The Spymaster taught us to heed such warnings. It told me something was wrong. While Hasha and Ann Mali said good-bye, I slipped out the door, silent as the spy I was.

Ducking behind the shrubs in front of their house, I waited. Ann Mali walked down the steps as Hasha's husband came running up, taking the steps two at a time. He opened the door and I heard him say, "Harn soldiers are massing south of the city. I fear they are coming to Namché. We need to take the girls and go up into the mountains."

In the Twelve Valleys, war was unknown but I dreaded an Army coming to the city. I sent a brief prayer to the Wind Goddess, asking for her protection. When I caught up with Ann Mali, I told her what I heard.

"He sounded certain an Army was coming. His words gave me a cold shiver."

"We will tell Mistress about this. She may forbid the Novices from coming to the city until we know more."

"What about me?" I hated the idea Mistress might ban me from working with Ann Mali. Being right about Hasha's baby gave me my first taste of success, and I found the work of preparing tinctures slow and tedious.

"Mistress will decide. Whatever she decides, Sab-ra, you will have to live with her decision."

As we climbed the hundred stairs, a nearly silent drum began to beat inside my head, like the sound of falling snow. It was if an enormous pulse counted the days before some cataclysmic event came roaring down the mountain and buried my life beneath an avalanche. I saw handfuls of seconds, minutes and days tumbling down the mountain crushing trees flat.

## Chapter 10 – The D-wali Child

The following afternoon, Ann Mali said we had a difficult situation to deal with. We walked down the stairs and beyond the barrier wall to the far outskirts of the city. I saw the entrance to the Wool Road and felt its pull, but Ann Mali grabbed my wrist tightly and said, "Come this way, Sab-ra."

She knocked on the door of a small wattle-and-daub house and an older woman appeared.

"I'm here for the baby," Ann Mali's voice sounded as if she were controlling her anger with difficulty.

"Just a moment and I'll get it," the woman responded and entered the house. We stood on the doorstep. I looked toward the horizon, feeling the call of the mountains.

"Stop thinking about leaving, Sab-ra," Ann Mali's voice was angry. "You wouldn't last a week without supplies. Focus on the patient we are going to see. Did you notice the woman didn't give the baby a name?"

Had she called the baby an *It*? I wondered.

When the woman reappeared, a teen-aged daughter hovered behind her. In her arms, she carried the smallest baby I had ever seen. The child was walnut brown with light hazel eyes. The baby made desperate faint cries.

"We haven't fed it in a whole day," the older woman sounded disgusted. "It refused to die."

Ann Mali took the baby and handed the wee one to me. I could almost fit the small body in my cupped hands. The teen-aged daughter pleaded with her mother, holding out her arms for the baby. The older woman responded harshly and slammed the door in our faces.

"The daughter was raped by a Kosi Warrior," Ann Mali told me as we walked away. "The girl's parents refused to accept a child of rape, especially one so malformed." She spoke in angry clipped tones. "They wanted to give the child to the Lamasery, but Maidenstone is no place for an infant. When we get back, we will decide what to do."

"Shouldn't we feed the small one," I asked. "The baby must be hungry." I felt deep sorrow for this little person, torn from her mother, hated by her grandmother. I identified with the child strongly. The child's cries continued until I put the tip of my smallest finger in the baby's mouth. The infant sucked strongly. I saw the tiny chest rising and falling in sleep.

We took the child up to the Infirmary and removed layers of bunting carefully, trying not to disturb her. The child was female. She had an average sized trunk. Her arms and legs were extremely short. Her fingers were also short with a wide separation between the middle and ring fingers. Her head seemed disproportionately large. She had severely bowed legs. In spite of these differences, or perhaps because of them, she was a winning little thing.

"What is wrong with her?" I whispered. The babe had gone back to sleep, and I didn't want to wake her.

"She's a dwarf, what the people of Namché call D-wali. The citizens of Namché consider them evil and cursed. There is no reason to kill her, except she would not be accepted anywhere."

Kill her! You weren't going to kill her, were you?" I was horrified. Anger rose searing hot inside me.

"It's what the grandmother wanted. They didn't want the baby's mother to encounter the child later in life. Perhaps the kindest thing would be to let her die. I can mix some Lethal Sleep in her bottle. She would fall asleep and never wake."

Rejected, starved and given away—the child gazed at us with calm intelligent eyes. I was infuriated Ann Mali would even consider taking the baby's life. My whole body blistered with anger.

"You can't give her poison," I shouted. Ann Mali looked startled by my loud declaration. "This baby wants to live. Is there no family that will accept her?"

"I have tried hard to find a place for her since she was born. Because she is a mixed breed, no family in the city will even foster her. There is an orphanage in the Twelve Valleys that will sometimes take unwanted children, but the matron won't usually take the misshapen D-wali."

"Could we ask Mistress if we could keep her at Maidenstone? I would take care of her."

"Sab-ra, you are not ready for such a responsibility. The D-wali baby would always be an outcaste; hated and shunned. It's a living death for these children."

"I will never let anyone give her a bottle filled with death!" I was shaking with fury. "I will take her back to Talin, against all the stupid rules of the Elders, rather than let her die."

"Sab-ra, your passion for this child warms me. Perhaps I can still come up with something. In the meantime, I promise you no one will give her a death bottle."

Walking back to my room, I suddenly recalled giving the Lethal Sleep berries to the People's woman stolen by the Kosi. I wondered if she ever poisoned the Warrior. Maybe she didn't. I had changed. I was so fierce in arguing for death for the Kosi Warriors, and now I was furious that Ann Mali would use the same poison on the baby D-wali.

Mistress called me to her office two days later. "Sab-ra, I have located an orphanage where the baby will be accepted." Elation lifted my soul. "But only if they receive a gift of significant value. I know your Grandfather gave you the Stars of Evening necklace as a reward for passing the Survival Test. Will you give your necklace to save the baby Dwali's life?"

I remembered the night Grandfather honored me with the jeweled band. A stab of loss made it hard to breathe. My eyes tingled with the onset of tears. The necklace was the only possession I had left from Talin, the symbol of all my hard work to become a spy. Grandfather told me to keep the necklace with me always, but compared to preventing a child's death, his wishes were meaningless. Of course, I would give the necklace away to save the baby's life.

Several days later, Conquin and I left Maidenstone surreptitiously in late afternoon. We were going to see the D-wali baby's mother. I sighed in relief when we found her alone, hanging out clothes to dry. She gave a harsh cry when she saw us and put her fist over her mouth. Dark hair blew across her forehead.

"Why are you here?" she cried. She seemed terrified.

"Don't worry. The baby is alive. She has gone to the Orphanage in the Twelve Valley's Kingdom. We named her Laelia."

The young woman nearly collapsed in relief. "I thank you, Mistresses," she bowed her head, tears in her eyes.

"You named her Lah-li?" She mispronounced the word but then corrected herself. "No, Laelia, like the flower. I like it."

"We call her Lia for short," I smiled, warming to this young mother. "What is your name?"

"It's Betiva."

"Do you mind telling us about Lia's father," I asked.

It took a moment for her to collect herself. Then she began.

"I was visiting my aunt in the mountains above the city when the Kosi kidnapped me. At first I was terrified, but I soon realized the Kosi were not what I had been told." She sounded perplexed, as if she couldn't believe what had happened to her.

"How did you return to your parents?" I was curious, needing this information for my mission, if I ever got another chance to retrieve our women.

"My uncle ransomed me, not realizing I was pregnant or was starting to feel like I belonged there." Her eyebrows lifted in surprise at the force of her own feelings. "The father of my baby was livid when the Chief of the tribe sold me back to my uncle."

Conquin reached out and touched the young woman gently on her shoulder, comforting her.

"Since my baby was born," Betiva continued, "I have thought many times about what my life would have been if I had stayed with the Kosi. The Kosi tribe love all babies and young children, especially the D-wali. The consider them to have the Far Seer gift. I wish my parents had left me there," her voice was bitter, "I miss my Warrior every day."

"The Orphanage will take good care of baby Lia, and perhaps when she is older, she could return to Namché and go to school here at Maidenstone. You could be back in her life," Conquin told her kindly and drew a circle blessing above Betiva's head.

Walking the pooling purple shadows back to school, Betiva's voice saying she wished her family had left her with the Warrior rang in my mind. She was so unhappy. I wanted to help her escape from her wretched mother.

"I wish Betiva could enter Maidenstone," I told Conquin.

"I doubt Mistress would take her. Her parents would not have the money to pay."

"Could we hide her do you think? She could live in one of the empty rooms at Maidenstone." I saw myself bringing food and bedding across the glass steps to the green tower.

"I think you should be brave enough to ask Mistress," Conquin told me, dryly.

"And I think you should be brave enough to go with me," I responded rolling my eyes at her, returning her challenge.


Although the hour was late, we knocked on Mistress Falcon's door and told her about Betiva.

"You just can't save everyone, Sab-ra," Mistress sounded exasperated. "Didn't you do enough, saving the baby?"

No, I didn't, I thought.

"Mistress, we lost our Laundress recently, didn't we?"

"Yes, Conquin, Maidenstone has little income at present. It's the reason why I can't take charity cases."

"Could Betiva do the laundry for the house?" I asked, hopefully. "She does the laundry for her mother who takes in washing."

"If you will stop trying to save the world, Sab-ra, I will talk with her," Mistress' voice was final. I flushed at her disapproval.

As we walked down the hall to our room, I took a deep breath. I had a confession to make to my best friend.

"Conquin, I have something I need to tell you."

"Don't tell me if you aren't ready, Sab-ra," she cautioned me.

"No, I am ready. I was banished from Talin because," I hesitated.

"Because of Hodi," she finished my sentence.

I stopped walking in shocked silence.

"You talk in your sleep about him. I know you want to avenge Hodi's death. You say the words Kosi Wolf and sometimes you punch your pillow."

I sighed deeply, feeling renewed pain at my failure to save Hodi.

"Ever since Hodi died, I planned to take the Kosi Wolf's life, but Jun said he wouldn't teach me until I gave up the revenge quest. He said I needed to find an honorable justice."

"Jun is right, but are you ready to give it away?"


Watching the moon as it rose outside our window after Conquin fell asleep, I knew I had to relinquish revenge. Jun would never give me the final Empath Test until I ceased to hunger for vengeance.

Using all the skills Jun had taught me, I created a small leather satchel in my mind. Then I picked up my wish for the Kosi Wolf's death, opened the satchel and put the desire for revenge deep inside. I locked the case with the spells the men of Talin used when they sealed the leather packs of Skygrass Stones. I gave my satchel wings and sent the valise flying over the foothills all the way up to the Skygrass Valley.

Looking out the window at the starlit sky, I took a deep breath and slowly my wish for vengeance departed. I saw it borne aloft, riding the winged suitcase.

## Chapter 11 - The Empath Test

Jun was waiting for me outside the dining room the next morning. He wore a red robe, signifying he was now a Monk.

"Congratulations Jun," I told him. He bowed to me.

"Are you ready now?" Jun asked me, silently.

"I am," I answered, also in silence.

"I see the satchel," his inward voice said and the corners of his mouth curved up. "Although you think you will open it one day, I tell you that satchel is locked for all time. You will find another way to honor Hodi's life."

I heaved a sigh and felt my shoulders relax. Hodi would have a reckoning someday, but revenge was unworthy of an Apprentice Healer who sought the Vermillion Cord. I would seek justice for Hodi on another path.

"Today you will take the Empath Test," Jun's smile filled me with pride.

I followed as Jun led me through the complex architecture of our school.

"The House of Maidenstone consists of three towers in an enormous compound we call the Lamasery. The novice towers—the red, yellow and orange ones—are only for women. The blue, turquoise and green towers complete the Lamasery. They are for Monks and their acolytes."

I wanted to seal everything about this day into my memory. I sensed whatever happened would be significant in the path of my life. A shiver of pleasure ran across my shoulders.

My footsteps were slow and careful on the clear glass steps until we reached the door to the white tower.

When we opened the door, we entered a six-sided room with windows on all sides. We stood upon a mezzanine, looking down into a vast light-filled space.

Two boys were painting a mural of dark pine trees and cranes. The depiction was so realistic I shivered, feeling the cool wind as it whistled through the bird's feathers. One panel showed only snow-covered pines. Jun told me the artist had painted eagles, but they were so real they flew off the canvas.

We walked downstairs to a sanctuary where the Monks intoned a low booming sound. There were hundreds of them, kneeling in the darkness. The bells of the monastery rang out repeatedly. The air was very cold. The trees in the courtyard below us had lost all their leaves.

"Conquin already passed her test. Did she tell you?" Jun asked.

I nodded.

"She succeeded brilliantly. I have devised a different test for you."

He led me down a hall with many doors. One stood open. Standing outside the door, I saw a member of the Bearer tribe. He wore a long knife in his red sash. We entered the room and saw a young acolyte lying on a bed. The boy's face was as white as the bed coverings. The room was starkly beautiful. The window looked out at the foothills, covered in drifting snow.

"This is Umbra," Jun said. "He is in a coma. He tried to kill himself by jumping into the White River, but an ice cutter pulled his body from the waters. I will leave you with him. Your must draw the story of why he wanted to end his life from his mind."

"When I know the story, what should I do then?"

"That is the second part of the test."

"What do you mean, Jun?"

"If you can pull the tale from his mind, your second test is to decide what you will do with that information." Jun bowed and left the room.

I sat on the bed beside the slim young man and took his sleeping hand in mine. I took his pulse. I placed my ear on his chest. Then I lowered my forehead to his.

"Umbra, will you tell me your story?" I asked him silently. I sat back and waited. His breathing quickened. Color came into his lips.

"The bad monk sent me to the soldiers' camp," he said, shaking his head from side to side.

I felt the beginnings of dread, just on the edges of my mind. It hovered like a dark cloud of Lakt. I remembered Hasha's husband saying soldiers were coming to Namché.

"Why did he send you?"

"To bring them the gold."

"What was the soldier going to do with gold?" I was controlling my voice with extreme difficulty, keeping it quiet, but my fears rose like dead leaves before the winter wind.

"Buy a cannon. He was going to obliterate the Yellow Tower."

My chest sank. I saw Mistress, the cooks, my beautiful room and Conquin lying broken in rubble.

Umbra began to weep. Tears came down his cheeks, but he didn't make a sound.

"I tied the gold bars to my chest. I dove into black water. I chose death. I shamed my father."

I wanted to help the fine young man who had been willing to die to keep Maidenstone safe. Remembering the guard outside Umbra's door, I realized he was probably there to prevent the bad monk from killing Umbra.

"You will wake now," I told him in a peaceful voice. His eyes flew open.

"I am Sab-ra of Maidenstone. I have learned the brave thing you did to save Maidenstone. We are in your debt. You must return home immediately. The Bearer outside the door will take you to your father."

Umbra's breathing quickened.

"Tell me the name of the bad monk. We will deal with him."

"I can't," his face turned white again.

"Umbra, you chose the coward's way when you jumped from the bridge. Now you must walk the true path."

He looked at me for a long time and then he whispered, "Brother Nierta. He said the old Abbott told him to destroy the Novices."

I kissed his forehead, told him to get dressed and left the room. I informed the Bearer that he would be taking Umbra home.

"Leave now," I told him. "Don't delay."

I needed to find Brother Jun and tell him what I had decided to do.

I didn't see Jun again for several weeks after the Test. Then one chilly morning as the huge snowflakes of late winter drifted past the windows of Maidenstone, I walked into the kitchen to see a monk standing by the stove. Wariness alerted me. Mistress Falcon only allowed Jun into our wing of the Lamasery. As the monk turned his face to me, I was jolted.

It was Brother Nierta. He held a pot of bubbling oil and jostled against me, spilling a single searing drop on my hand. My recognition came simultaneously with the scream of pain that rose in my throat.

---

"You know who I am, don't you," he said fiercely.

I turned my face away but he grabbed my chin, pulling my eyes back to his.

"I will pour this burning oil on your face. I will scar you like the Yeti of the mountains if you tell Mistress my plan."

"I told her already," I said ferociously. I clenched my teeth and wrenched my chin away. I bit the inside of my mouth, feeling the pain, tasting the blood.

"I told them all."

As Brother Nierta raised the container of hot oil, we heard footsteps. Looking over Brother Nierta's shoulder, I saw the Headman of Namché, Jun and Brother Marzun enter the room with Mistress. The Headman tied Brother Nierta's hands behind his body. Brother Nierta looked at me in a blazing rage. His fury made sweat break out on my forehead. A piercing pain hit me behind my eyes. A black cloud settled on my mind like ink spreads in water.

I woke in the Infirmary to Ann Mali rubbing salve gently on my hand. I could see sunset clouds from the windows. I had slept away an entire day. My confrontation with Brother Nierta had taken all my reserves of energy. Weakness covered my spirit. A blanket of heavy cool sand seemed to lay over me.

It was almost dark when Brother Jun entered the Infirmary saying, "Walk with me."

I stood up, a little unsteadily and followed him. My hand was still sore. He took me to the Teaching Room. Conquin was already there.

"You have both conquered the Empath Test." Joy lit his face. "Sab-ra, you are to be rewarded today. Conquin, your reward will be born in the spring," he grinned at her.

"*Born* in the spring?" she asked, sounding excited and pleased.

We walked down the hall to Mistress Falcon's office. She called us inside. At a nod from Jun, she reached into a dark wooden cabinet and laid two shining Indigo Cords, symbolizing the fully trained Empath, on her desk.

"You are now both Entitled Empaths," she smiled. "We are proud of you. From this day forward, you will never remove your Cords, except for bathing. The work of the Empath will always be with you. I ask you now to swear the Oath. Say the words after me."

"I will do my best for those who come to me.

"I will never judge or threaten a patient.

"I will never reveal a person's secrets.

"I will take away their pain."

Hands on hearts, we pledged. Deeply impressed with the significance of the Oath, Conquin and I stood tall while Jun and Mistress tied the elaborate Indigo Cords around our waists.

Tiny snowflakes fell on our hair and shoulders as we walked across the high turquoise bridge in the darkness. The air was so cold I could see my breath. A small tree grew below us in the courtyard, its branches bare. Currents of air sent sheets of snow skittering across the open space. An acolyte in a yellow robe was calling a small dog. We descended a staircase and walked into a room where he held the dog for us to see. She was white with yellow ears. I had never seen such a dog. The dogs in my country are large, black and lunging. They will bite without provocation and carry disease.

"How beautiful she is," I exclaimed laughing. "Her ears are like flags." I was enchanted.

Jun smiled at my reaction. "Her name is Saki, but there is more. Come with me."

We walked into an adjacent room where I saw a bed draped in tangerine silk. One dim lamp lit the darkness. The acolyte placed the dog on the bed beside four small puppies. One was white. The others were brown, black and yellow. All were very young, their eyes still closed.

I sat on the bed and asked Saki silently if I could touch her newborns. She gazed at me trustingly. I picked one up. He was a miniature of his mother, tiny and pure white with ivory colored ears. A dark spot in the corner of his eyes showed me when his eyes opened they would be black. I yearned to hold him tight to my chest. I ached to feel his tiny heartbeat.

"You may choose one of the puppies for yourself," Jun told me.

"He is the heart of a cloud," I said and my spirit filled with joy.

"He is yours and will be called Cloudheart. All of Saki's children are Temple dogs, sacred animals who serve the Monks living here. You must guard him carefully. The monks have given you a rare gift, Sab-ra. I have never known a Novice to receive one before today.

"Cloudheart is not old enough to leave Saki yet," Jun said, "But you can come and visit him. In a few more weeks, he will be ready to live in the Novice towers. You must teach him to sit quietly when you study, walk beside you when you go to Namché and guard your sleep."

Cloudheart would become my new partner. I would keep him with me always. The monks had given me a second chance, something the Elders of Talin wouldn't do.

On the day the monks said I could take Cloudheart to Maidenstone, I carried him home in my hands and he last vestiges of my loneliness lifted. The black Lakt within me rose and flew away toward the dark mountains. I saw them disappear and felt the sun shine down on my life, enormous and golden.

Yet still in the back of my mind, the distant snow-drum beat.

## Chapter 12 – Cloudheart Goes Missing
## Long Night Moon, 12<sup>th</sup> month

Receiving the Indigo Cord renewed my passion to become a recognized Healer and earn the Vermillion Cord. I returned to the Infirmary, preparing medicines with increased care. A few days later, a young Novice handed me a note from Ann Mali. She was ready to go to the city. There was an emergency. I dashed down the stairs. I wanted to check on Cloudheart before I left.

Recently he had been stalking voles. He smelled them under the snow and dug them out. I worried he would chase one beyond the stacked-stone walls of the kitchen garden and get lost. He was my new partner, and I had vowed to keep him safe.

"Stay," I told Cloudheart, leaving him in the hall outside the door to my room. I wasn't sure he had learned the command perfectly. I feared I hadn't spent enough time teaching him. When I turned back, he was sitting just outside the door, hunched and dejected looking. I couldn't leave him like that.

"Come, Cloudheart," I called. He lifted his face, smiling. We searched for Conquin and found her working with the cooks in the kitchen.

"I have to go to the city, Conquin. Will you watch Cloudheart for me? If you leave the kitchen to go outside, will you put a leash on him? It's easier to catch him that way."

Ann Mali waited in the front entry, obviously irritated by my delay.

"You are late, Sab-ra. We are seeing Gordo's child, Malau, this morning. They said we were needed urgently."

We hurried down the mountain to Gordo's large house.

Gordo was the gem merchant in Namché who organized the sale of the People's Skygrass Stones. Their home was beautiful, light and airy. Statues of the golden god stood in every room.

Gordo's wife Ken-dra was distraught with worry about their oldest daughter, Malau. The little girl was only six. She had a high fever, a spotty rash and the inside of her mouth was bright red. There were white spots on her lips. Her breath smelled acrid.

"It is the Rhia sickness?" I whispered to Ann Mali.

"Hush, Sab-ra," she frowned. Then she whispered, "You are correct but don't tell Ken-dra or Gordo the name of this disease. They know Rhia is fatal. When will you learn, Sab-ra, in matters of health, hope is more important than truth."

I had no idea what she meant. I wanted to care for patients on my own by then. Ann Mali was no longer a well-loved teacher; she was an irritant, a barrier standing in my way. Gone were the days when I sought her approval. I had not felt the Lakt of my failures for a long time. I presumed them gone for good.

After bathing the child in tepid water, we asked whether we could take her with us to the Infirmary, but the parents refused.

"I fear Malau has the summer Rhia fever," Ann Mali told Ken-dra. Both of Malau's parents paled.

She told me I couldn't share this information and then she did. I was infuriated.

"If an epidemic comes, you must bring her to Maidenstone. If she coughs up blood, bring her immediately."

Clinging to her husband, Ken-dra stood in the open doorway to their lovely house, desperately praying to the golden god to spare her child.

As we walked away, my mouth tightened.

———

"Why did you tell Gordo and Ken-dra that Malau had Rhia, but when I whispered the name of the disease, you told me to be quiet?" The heat of anger flared in my tightened belly.

"I didn't want to tell them the name of the disease, but once they decided we could not take her with us, I thought they should know. If Malau is the first case, we might stop the epidemic at this point. We might even save her, if they bring her to Maidenstone soon enough." Her voice was heavy with apprehension.


When Ann Mali and I reached the forecourt at Maidenstone, Mistress Falcon and Jun were waiting. The terrible desolation emanating from them rocked against me. Jun touched my forehead and a flood of images me hit like a storm of ice. He showed me an acolyte monk running away from Maidenstone. I saw Cloudheart dash after him. Wild Ghat migrated in large groups up the mountain. Cloudheart ran close behind their heels. His leash, still attached, made a tiny road in the dust.

Jun began, "Our youngest acolyte, Timbe, ran away to rejoin his family. He climbed the garden wall with Cloudheart in his arms. Conquin caught a glimpse of them leaving and ran outside. She dashed through the gate, trying desperately to stop them."

Fear clutched my heart like a claw.

"Oh no, please no," I covered my mouth with my hands.

"Conquin fell into the river by some jagged rocks," Jun said. "She fainted and for a long time we could not find her. She is in the Infirmary asking for you. I am sorry, Sab-ra, but there was no sign of Cloudheart."

I felt desolation in every breath I took. I had felt such pain only once before, when I saw Hodi tied to the Kosi tree. My throat constricted. I could not speak.

I didn't want to see Conquin; I was furious she had let Cloudheart escape. I ran up to our room, collapsed on my bed and lay convulsed in sobs. Conquin returned late in the evening. She had a wrapped bandage on her wrist. Her face was pale as clay. When she opened the door, I was sitting on my bed fighting tears. Cloudheart's sleeping sack lay on the floor between our beds.

Conquin picked up his sack, holding the furry softness against her chest. When she turned to look at me, her eyes were wet.

"I am so sorry, Sab-ra," she broke down in sobs.

Seeing how wretched she felt, I stood and hugged her. I wanted Cloudheart back with every cell in my body, but Conquin's remorse was so profound, I had to forgive her.

We studied for a while, but I could not concentrate. I was desperate to distract myself from Cloudheart's disappearance.

"I can't focus on this, can you?" I asked.

"No, not really."

"I have to do something to stop myself thinking about Cloudheart. I want to search for him but it's already dark. Mistress insisted we stay inside until morning." I got up and prowled around our room. "Conquin, the only thing I can think of is to go to the monk's towers. Maybe we can see Cloudheart from up there, and I've wanted to explore those towers for months."

"Sab-ra, we're not supposed to go over there."

"I know we're not, but the upper floors are completely empty. It's just one of those stupid rules for no reason. Let's go, please Conquin?"

Although Conquin was reluctant, I finally convinced her. We grabbed our coats, left our room and tiptoed down the corridor, careful no other Novices heard us. We opened the door leading to the green bridge tower and felt the icy wind.

"Come on." Conquin looked so guilty that I laughed. I led her by the hand.

Crossing the glass steps was always a trial of courage but especially at night. When we reached the door into the green tower, we were surprised to find it unlocked. Once inside, we walked down hall after hall. The silent trespassing recalled my spying skills, and I found to my relief my mind was able to focus on the task.

Many rooms had built-in cabinets for linens or religious artifacts, but sometimes at the back of a cabinet, there was another door. We crawled into several of these only to find ourselves in other rooms. Most were empty, dusty with old furniture. We wondered if they were tiny hiding places.

In one of the interior rooms, we heard monks talking. Our Empath skills let us take pictures from their minds. We saw monks taken prisoner and images of uniformed marching men. We saw public hangings and soldiers executing prisoners by firing squad. It was a time we believed would never touch us in peaceful Namché.

"I think they are seeing the future," I told Conquin, frowning at the images.

"Do you think a war is coming?" Conquin whispered. "Didn't one of your patients say an Army was approaching?"

"Yes, but the Bearer people told Mistress the Army had retreated. Still, sometimes I feel it coming." The distant drum in my mind quickened, like a second beating heart.

"I hate to think of the devastation a war would bring. So many deaths," Conquin's voice was sad. "What do your People believe happens after a person dies, Sab-ra?"

"We believe if a person has done something of permanent good, they will walk the Great Dhali Ra Mountain forever."

"I don't know if I want to live forever," Conquin frowned. "It seems to me we try to do our best because our time here is short."

"I would like to do something that would last forever," I told her wistfully. "If I could, perhaps I would be remembered after my body has joined the earth."

"Only Kings are remembered after they die," Conquin said.

As we walked on, I mused for the first time about what I could do for my People, beyond locating our women in the camps of the Kosi. I dreamed of a way to end the violence, the kidnapping, spying and killing. Without a lasting peace between the People and the Kosi, the devastation would never end. The People would become extinct and the mythic Skygrass valley would be a Paradise for none.

In the last room we investigated, I saw a trap door on the floor. Lifting the golden ring attached to the lid, we spotted a small wooden chest. Inside we saw heavy golden bars.

"Conquin, I want to take this to Mistress," I said excitedly. "She told us she needs money for Maidenstone."

"No, Sab-ra. We should leave this where we found it."

"I think Mistress would be pleased," insistence made my voice loud.

"I don't think so, Sab-ra," Conquin's face was severe. "You know we shouldn't even be in the monk's tower. We need to go back now."

"In a minute," I told her.

She looked at me, shook her head and said, "I'm leaving now."

I walked to the window and looked down, hoping for a glimpse of a little white dog in a blowing white snowdrift, but nothing moved. Lifting my eyes, I saw Conquin already crossing the bridge to the yellow tower. I picked up the chest and lugged it down the hall. I wanted Mistress to have the gold. I wanted to see her smile.

Then the hairs on the back of my neck rose. I felt something menacing. An evil presence watched me. I ran awkwardly toward the door, hampered by the weight of the chest. I kept glancing behind me, feeling a brooding malevolence.

In my mind, I heard, "Novices pollute this holy place."

I shoved my shoulder against the green door. It flew open. Cold air and snow blasted my face. I tightened my grip on the trunk and stepped onto the glass bridge. The horror grew stronger. Then I saw him. It was a hooded monk in a dark brown habit. He had no features—only a shadow lived inside the garment. His image wavered and vanished, but I could feel him still beside me. My heart thumped fast as a racing pony.

"Help me," I screamed. "Conquin, help me."

Conquin was almost across the bridge. She was heaving open the door to the yellow tower. The wind was so strong she lost her footing. She grabbed for the glass steps, screaming in fear. Her upper body rested on the step, but from the waist down, she dangled in the air. I was terrified the wind would push her off. The monk's cold hand grabbed my wrist.

"Goddess, stop the wind," I shrieked and the screaming wind fell silent. Conquin scrambled to her feet. She began to run toward me. A black hand forced the chest from my grasp. The chest broke open, spilling golden bars on green glass steps.

Conquin reached me, grabbed my arm and dragged me onto the bridge. Part way across, out of breath, we turned around. Golden bars, hundreds and thousands of them fell infinitely slowly through the wintry night. We never heard them strike the stones below. A black hand closed the door to the monk's keep.

I was trembling violently. "Did you see a monk, Conquin?"

"No," she seemed confused, "But I heard you calling."

"It was an evil thing, not fully human," I shuddered again, seeing the faceless hood and feeling the cold hand.

I wished we had never gone to the Monk's Tower.

"What made you turn around?"

"I felt your fear. The wind was dreadfully strong, but when it stopped, I was able to get to my feet. You seemed to be struggling with something. When you turned toward me, I saw a thousand golden bars tumble down into the mist."

We walked across the bridge in silence. Just as we entered the yellow door, Conquin tilted her head to one side and remarked, "We have never been able to reach each other's thoughts across an air bridge before. I wonder how far our thoughts can travel."

My own wondering went in a different direction. I remembered Grandfather saying, "My son could call the wind."

Had I called the wind? Had I inherited my father's powers? How I wanted some trace of him to be alive in me.


I went directly to Mistress Falcon's office the next morning. Unlike my escapes to the rooftops of Maidenstone, when I wasn't sure I was doing anything wrong, entering the Monk's Towers was expressly forbidden. I was breathing fast, knowing I had to tell her but dreading her reaction. I only went because I was desperate to stop thinking about Cloudheart. I sat down in the chair opposite her beautifully carved desk.

"What is it, Sab-ra?" Mistress asked, sounding tired.

"Conquin and I went across the green bridge into the monk's quarters last night. I had to do something to keep from thinking about Cloudheart. I hoped to spot him from the windows of the green tower."

"Sab-ra," Mistress folded her arms across her chest. "I told you the day you started here that the green, blue and turquoise towers belonged to the Monks. Novices are not permitted to go across those bridges."

I nodded, "I know."

Mistress' voice was serious. "Tell me what happened."

"I found a small chest of golden bars in one of the last rooms."

Mistress seemed captivated by my words. "The treasure," she murmured.

"I wanted to bring you the gold, to help you with Maidenstone. I walked toward the door carrying it but a shadowy monk started wrestling with me. He was trying to take it away."

There was a long silence before Mistress spoke. "Let me tell you a little history of this remarkable place, Sab-ra. The first citizens of Namché built the Lamasery hundreds of years ago on the ruins of an ancient monastery. The monks welcomed the new buildings, but when they learned Novices would be coming here, the Abbott was enraged. He forced the other monks to tear down the stonework at knifepoint. He believed women would pollute his holy place.

"Every day the builders built up a few rows of the women's towers and every night monks tore them down. The situation came to a head and the Abbott's reign of terror ended. No one knows whether he killed himself, was killed by the builders or was entombed alive in the stonework. Many of the monks say they have seen the old Abbott's ghost. He refused to wear the new red robes and held to the old brown homespun. They told me the color of his skin was black."

"It was. I saw his hand."

"I saw him once," she seemed lost in the memory. "He was crossing the turquoise bridge toward the yellow tower. The wind was blowing hard but didn't stir his robe. When I became Mistress here, the oldest monk told me every Mistress of Maidenstone sees him."

"What did you whisper earlier; something about treasure?"

"When the largest Monastery in the land sent gold bars to pay for the building of the Novice towers, the crazed Abbott hid the chest somewhere in the Monk's quarters. The monks searched everywhere after the Abbott died, but the gold was never recovered."

"Brother Nierta must have found it because he gave Umbra some of the gold. He said the old Abbott wanted Umbra to give the gold to a soldier who would destroy the Yellow tower."

"So many centuries after the Abbott's death, yet his insanity still found its way into the mind of Brother Nierta," she sighed.

"Will he ever be released from the city prison do you think? He frightens me."

"Never while I rule Maidenstone," she said in a solemn voice. "Sab-ra, by going to the Monk's towers, you have ignored the rules again. I can't keep punishing you, only to have you disregard my guidance. I have come to the reluctant realization that rules will not control you. Putting you back into the cell won't work either. I hate to do this, but I am out of options. Hold out your hand."

I hesitated, fearing what she would do. Mistress handed me a tiny knife. Its blade was sharp-honed steel.

"Cut across your right palm." Her voice was harsh.

I tried not to show the pain as I cut into my palm.

"Deeper."

I made a long deep cut. Despite myself, I cried out at the end. I held my wrist up to keep the blood from dripping on the floor. Mistress handed me a piece of linen to quench the bleeding.

"Was the idea of going into the monk's towers yours or Conquin's."

"It was mine, Mistress."

"Go to the Infirmary. After you are bandaged, bring Conquin here."

When we returned, Mistress took Conquin into her office and made me wait in the hall. I was frantic to hear what was happening. I could not let Mistress punish Conquin for my stupid idea.

After a long time, Conquin opened the door and motioned for me to enter. Her face was bloodless.

"Sab-ra, Conquin concurs with your story, but since she agreed to go with you, she must also be punished."

"Take my knife," Mistress' voice was trembling as if she forced herself to say the words, "Cut Conquin's palm."

My stomach roiled. "Mistress, the whole misguided adventure was my idea, I should be punished."

"You heard me, Sab-ra, cut Conquin's palm."

Conquin held out her hand to me. She shuddered and turned her face away. I heard a soft sob. I touched the tip of the knife gently to the center of her palm. Her supple little hand just did me in. I heaved the knife to the floor.

"I will not do this," I told Mistress through my tears and rage.

To my surprise, Mistress took a deep breath saying, "I wanted to find out if you would cut your friend. I am pleased to see you would not. However, if you cross any of the monk's bridges again, I will force you to cut Conquin, even if I have to hold your hand on the knife."

We were all quiet for a few moments and then Mistress spoke.

"Before you go, girls, I have one other thing to tell you. It's a good thing," she smiled. "Betiva is going to be Maidenstone's new laundress. When she has time between her duties, I will teach her to read. Sab-ra, you can help me."

Conquin and I met each others eyes and relief flashed between us.

## Chapter 13 – The Epidemic

Ann Mali and I returned to Gordo and Ken-dra's house the next morning. Knowing Malau had contracted the Rhia fever, I wanted to convince them to let us take her to Maidenstone. I was certain I could be more persuasive than Ann Mali was. I worried Malau's little brother and sister would contract Rhia if we didn't get the six-year-old to the Infirmary.

The River Goddess was breaking up the ice in the White River. Loud cracks from shattering slabs filled the air. The men of Namché stood on small barges in the black rocking waters and caught sheets of ice with long silver pinchers. They stored the ice between layers of sawdust in special buildings. Meat and milk sellers purchased the ice to keep their goods from spoiling.

We heard the horrible cries of mourning before we entered Gordo's home. Malau had died in the night. I wrapped my arms around Ken-dra, feeling her wretchedness. Gordo put his arms around their other two children. Unless we treated them immediately, they would be next.

"Please get your younger children ready to go," Ann Mali ordered.

This time there was no protest.

"It is as I feared," she whispered to me. "You have never lived through an epidemic. The harsh sound of the ice cutters on the river will be nothing compared to the broken cries of the parents of dying children."

Ann Mali asked Gordo and Ken-dra to tell everyone to bring their children to Maidenstone at the first sight of a sore throat or any child who coughed up blood.

I picked up their baby son, feeling my heart clench in fear. We took the two children to the Infirmary and told Mistress the Rhia fever had claimed its first victim. Fear of the Rhia's power made me clench my fists.

I was determined to save Malau's brother and sister.

"Gather all the Novices in the forecourt," Mistress told us. The planes of her face seemed carved in stone.

All of us stood waiting for Mistress Falcon's instructions.

"The children of Namché have the Rhia fever," she announced. "We will need all of you, even those who have not trained as Healers, to help fight this epidemic. In the next few days, we will first see only a trickle of parents carrying children up the hundred stairs. Then the trickle will become a torrent. Pray your youth and strength will protect you from the fever. Usually no one succumbs once reaching adolescence.

"Here are the assignments. Conquin, I know you have just started learning about medicines, but you will be in charge of the Medicine Table in the Infirmary. Only three extracts are of any help. We will need hundreds of vials prepared."

"I?" Conquin blanched, "I will be in charge?"

"Yes," Mistress told her, coolly. "You will supervise Ange and Lanel who will collect as much plant material as they can find. We will need feverfew, rose hips and any pearls of the Poppy you can locate."

Ange and Lanel's eyes grew large with alarm.

"Perced and Ryle, you will be responsible to help triage the children as they arrive. You will stand in the forecourt of Maidenstone and assess each patient. Ann Mali will tell you what to watch for. Brother Jun and Brother Marzun will set up tents and beds there. You will carry all children who are not in the throes of death up to the Infirmary."

Perced reached for Ryle's hand. She gripped it so tightly; I saw Ryle's hand turn white.

"Your legs will be so sore you will you want to perish. You will feel desperate to sink into even the filthiest bed, but you will not do it. Remember, every child you carry to the Infirmary has a chance. Every dose of medicine can save a life. You alone can open the doors to life or slam them shut."

All the Novices wore grave faces. This was a momentous time in our lives and all of us knew it.

"Betiva, you will need help in the laundry. Go into town, and bring as many women as you can to help you. They must bring bushels of soap grasses. Once they enter Maidenstone, they will not be leaving until the last child departs alive or is given to the outcastes for burial."

The color drained from Betiva's face as she nodded.

"You will be one of the most important people fighting this fever," Mistress' voice was kind, "and I have given you the worst job. Every day you will walk up three flights of stairs to the Infirmary. You will take the sheets, which will be black with diarrhea, yellow with vomit and red with blood down to the laundry.

"You will wash the linens, dry them in the sun and return fresh bedding to the Infirmary. You will do this a thousand times before the epidemic is over. May the Goddess bless your work and preserve your life."

Awe washed Betiva's face. She seemed uplifted by the chance to help the children. Perhaps she saw her service as a way to thank the Goddess for protecting little Lia, safe in the Twelve Valleys Orphanage.

"Sab-ra, for the duration of the epidemic you will be Lead Healer. You will take Ann Mali's place in the city. She is needed here to treat the children. Adults do not die of the Rhia but they get very sick. None of them can come to Maidenstone. Some may threaten, bribe or coerce you. You cannot give in. We barely have enough room for the children."

Panic roared across my mind. What if I forgot everything Ann Mali had taught me? I took a deep breath, trying to compose myself.

"What about Hasha?" I asked. "She is almost ready to deliver."

Mistress consulted briefly with Ann Mali. "Bring all four of her daughters here immediately. When she starts into labor, you will deliver the child at their home. She and the baby can remain there for two days. Then both of them must come here. It's the only chance her baby has."

Goddess, grant me the skill to be the Healer Ann Mali has trained me to be, I prayed.

"Like the washerwomen or the kitchen help, once Hasha is here, she will not leave until the fight against the Rhia is over. Get your medical bag, Sab-ra; make sure you have all your supplies. Go now."

I hesitated, wanting to hear all of Mistress Falcon's instructions.

"We need food and more cooks than Honus and Kieta," Mistress continued. "I will send them to scour the city for supplies and assistants. Ann Mali will show all of you how to make bandages. We will tear up the novice gowns for this purpose."

"What will we wear then, Mistress?" Ange asked looking around at all of us garbed in pristine white.

"We have white aprons in the kitchen. Wear them over the clothes you came here wearing. This will be a test for all of you, a test of your courage and your compassion."

When she stopped talking, a buzz of fearful conversation hovered over the forecourt, like a swarm of bees. I saw Monks walking the glass bridges, carrying beds on their backs to the Infirmary. We helped them put the beds in the halls, stacked them atop other beds like bunks and shoved them in every open room.

After the beds were stowed, I left for Hasha's house, dashing down the precipitous stairs. The drumbeat in my mind was louder than ever. I partially closed my eyes, squinting to allay the headache that stabbed my temples. Knowing how quickly the Rhia claimed its victims, I ran recklessly. I was determined to save Hasha's daughters.

The next morning, the first parents ascended the hundred steps.


I spent my days going from house to house in the city, forcibly taking children from their weeping parents, bandaging wounds, tending the old. Most adults would not accept my help. They told me to return to Maidenstone, to care for the children there. Whenever I finished my work in the city, I climbed the hundred steps and the three floors to the Infirmary asking, "What can I do?"

We all soothed small fevered heads with cool cloths, spooned broth into children's mouths, stripped beds of soiled linen and carried fresh linen upstairs. When small children survived, Ann Mali put them to work until their parents could claim them. Even five-year-olds carried food up and down the stone steps. When I saw them, I straightened my back and kept working. If such little ones could help, I would not sleep. For four weeks, no one did.

Once I arrived in the laundry with dirty sheets and was shocked to have them taken by Betiva's mother, the woman I'd hated when she rejected little Lia.

"You were right," she whispered to me, "I was wrong. May the Goddess forgive me, for I cannot forgive myself."

Another late night, I was comforting a crying child when I saw Mistress on her hands and knees, scrubbing vomit from the floor of the Infirmary. As she crawled over to the next bed, her knees left small bloody prints on the once clean floor.

I drew her body upright and took her place. "Sleep," I told her, seeing her eyes close as she leaned against me. "Just sleep."

The only time I ever felt a slight lightening of my spirit was the day Hasha's son was born. She had delivered healthy children before. I expected no problems. Her labor lasted many hours and pain crested over her in waves, but true to her cheerful nature, Hasha never once cried out.

When she crowned, I cupped my hands to receive her son's small slippery body. For a short time as we bathed and examined him, my spirit was at peace.

In four weeks, the Rhia fever burned through the city like a forest fire. The outcastes took the children's bodies away day and night through the side door of Maidenstone. Black-clad Priestesses drew final blessings over small dead bodies. They could have been ospreys bending over prey. The line of parents climbing the stairs with children reached all the way down to the Leopard Gate. Brother Jun carried water to them hourly and prayed for their children's lives.

Over a hundred children died of the Rhia. Many were with us for such a short time; I did not even learn their names. I was elated when I found out Phin had recovered. He was my first patient. One young orphan, Deti, also miraculously survived. She had no parents to claim her so Ann Mali immediately put her to work. Mistress agreed to keep her as a Novice when the Epidemic was over.

Gordo and Kendra's two younger children lived and I rejoiced. Hasha's little daughters all died. I blamed myself incessantly for delaying long enough to help put beds into rooms before running to their house. Hasha never murmured a word of censure. Instead, she thanked me many times for her son's life. Guilt lashed my heart. She named her baby boy Stone, in honor of Maidenstone. At least I had saved him.

Bells rang from every temple. The whole city mourned.

# Chapter 14 – Cloudheart's Return
## Moon of Snows, 1st Month

We had entered the Moon of Snows the day we learned a sawmill accident on the outskirts of Namché left a dozen men with dangling toes or missing fingers. Ann Mali came into the city to assist me. She and I sewed up flaps of skin and bandaged cuts for grateful lumberjacks. While we worked, an ice storm blanketed the misty city, leaving moisture on the cobbled streets. When we finished with the last patient, we headed for the hundred steps.

Cloudheart's disappearance had visited me seldom during the Epidemic, but that evening his face returned with a knife-like intensity. Approaching the stone steps in the shining dusk, I saw him alone in the bleak mountains or eaten by a mountain leopard. Tears closed my eyelids. I prayed with every ounce of my spirit for his safe return to Maidenstone.

In the dusk, I spotted a small child. She was headed toward us, but when she saw Healers from Maidenstone, she whirled around and dashed away. She carried a wiggling little bundle in her arms. Although the sky was nearly dark, I knew that little bundle—it was Cloudheart.

"Cloudheart," I called. He raised his head up and tried to look over the girl's shoulder. She pulled his head down against her. I whirled around, intent on following them, but Ann Mali grabbed my arm and stopped me.

"Sab-ra, that wasn't Cloudheart. How many times have you seen him in your mind? Come with me."

I was torn. My hard-won obedience warred with my desperation to recover my pet. At first, I turned to follow Ann Mali. She was so sure I would do what she told me, she didn't even look back. If I didn't obey her, Mistress would exact a terrible punishment.

"Stop Mistress," I reached to touch her shoulder.

"Please stop. I didn't see a spirit dog. I saw Cloudheart's face. I must follow them."

"Obey me, Sab-ra. Walk with me now."

I could not give in this time. The light was fading. The child and the dog had already vanished. A momentary qualm shook me. Could I have seen another visitation, another spirit dog? No, something was different.

"Mistress Physician, I beg you to release me. I must learn whether he is alive."

"Sab-ra, he is gone." Her tone was strident. "Your pride has been your downfall many times. If you fail to obey me, you risk dismissal from Maidenstone."

A terrible wrench tore my body, ripping my heart in half.

"I cannot," I sobbed and dashed down the slippery stairs.

"Sab-ra," I heard her angry voice cry out.

I turned away from the steps. The Wind Goddess herself blew me down the right path. After frantic minutes looking down each street, I saw the child's shadow as she darted into the alcove of a closed doorway. I reached in and grabbed her skinny shoulder. I dragged her struggling into the street. She set Cloudheart down. Clamping my hands around her wrist, to prevent her escape, I knelt down. I had to be sure it was my puppy.

"Oh Cloudheart, how I have missed you," I murmured. I lifted him in my arms, tears burning. He was thin, but his eyes still sparkled. His soul was intact. Pleasure roared through my veins, and the Lakt of my failures hung their heads. Cloudheart had returned. I let go of the girl's wrist, but to my surprise, she didn't run away. Cloudheart stood quietly between us.

"He is not yours. He is mine," she was gasping for breath. "He doesn't love you."

She stood with her hands on her tiny hips, looking furious and undaunted. I almost laughed at her ferocity but dampened my impulse.

"Please don't take him, he loves me," she begged. She was so small, dressed in tatters. She smelled of wheat flour, probably from begging for bread among the food sellers.

I reached for Cloudheart, but he stepped toward her. What was happening here? Didn't he belong to me? I picked him up, but he squirmed to get down. Holding on to Cloudheart, I grabbed her arm.

"Come with me." I was furious with this little urchin, this dirty kidnapper. Like the Kosi, she had taken my beloved.

"Where is your family?"

"Near the third valley."

"What is your name?"

"Tol Mec."

"I am Sab-ra." I could tell she was desperately poor.

"Where did you get this dog?"

"I have kept him safe from the kitchens for many weeks," she responded proudly. She saw I was puzzled and added, "They wanted to cook him, to eat him."

Horror took my mind. No one among my People or at Maidenstone ate the meat of any animal that nursed its young, but I knew the poor sometimes resorted to dog meat. Cloudheart, a sacred Temple dog, cooked and eaten? Goddess, save him.

"When did you find him?"

"It was the middle of the Long Night Moon."

She named the day Cloudheart had run away. This wretched little abductor had kept him safe for months.

"I found him running in the mountains above the big Lamasery. He wanted to come with me."

"What do you call him, little one?" I asked her, more gently.

"I call him, Trésor." It was the People's word for treasure.

At his new name, Cloudheart struggled in my arms. I set him down. He walked over to Tol Mec's feet and licked her toes.

"Come with me." I pulled the little wretch behind me. I dragged her down the street, struggling and fighting. Refusing to release her, I walked all three of us up the hundred steps to Maidenstone. She wasn't going to escape with Cloudheart again. Entering by the front door, completely unmoved by her whispered pleas and prayers, I marched her into the kitchen.

Mistress Falcon was waiting with Ann Mali. Both of them lifted furious eyes to me.

"I beg your forgiveness, Ann Mali and Mistress." When neither responded, I continued. "I have brought Tol Mec here. She has had Cloudheart since the day he disappeared. In fact," I took a deep breath, "despite her own hunger, she saved his life from people who would have eaten him. He comes to the new name she has given him. Oh, Mistress Falcon, what am I to do?" I sat at the table, lowered my head on my hands and sobbed, praying for her forgiveness.

Ann Mali rose, beckoned to Tol Mec and led her from the room. Cloudheart hesitated, running back and forth between us until he finally settled near my feet.

"Sab-ra," Mistress Falcon's angry voice brought me to my senses. "You have disobeyed a direct order from your teacher. You have been stubborn and disobedient. What punishment is appropriate for this?"

"The cell," I responded, feeling wretched. I dreaded the evil smiles of the Lakt in my mind that guarded the door.

"Oh, I don't think the cell will be enough this time," her voice was low. I raised my eyes to her, very afraid. "This time I am going to ask you. What do you think your punishment should be?"

"I don't know," I wailed. I started to sob again.

"Go to your room."

"Can I take Cloudheart with me?" I begged through my tears.

"No. Cloudheart will live in the kitchen until I decide what to do with you."

Mistress had asked me to name my punishment. I lay awake all night thinking. By morning, I knew. The only punishment I thought Mistress might accept would be giving Cloudheart away. My footsteps rang on the cold stone floor as I walked the long hall to Mistress Falcon's office. I kept reminding myself that what mattered most was having Cloudheart safe. I would give him back to the Monks, to the Cooks, to Mistress herself. I would do anything to keep him at Maidenstone alive, fed and loved. I had an idea what to do about Tol Mec, also. She was so far from family. She needed to stay here with us. I knocked on the door and at Mistress' command, opened it.

"Sab-ra, what am I to do with you?"

"I believe I know," I was surprised to see her lips tug reluctantly into a smile.

"Tell me."

"If I were Mistress of Maidenstone, I would keep Tol-mec here. I am sure she is already clean, fed and her sores treated. I would make her a Novice to see what Maidenstone would burn away from her character and what bright self would emerge."

"I see," her voice was calm with a touch of irony. "I thought the epidemic burned all the dross from your bright self, until Ann Mali told me you failed to do as she directed last night. I know you served as Lead Healer during the Rhia epidemic, Sab-ra, but she is now your teacher again. I asked you to tell me what your punishment should be."

"I think I must give Cloudheart away, but giving him to a child from Namché or back to the Monks will not work. I would seek him constantly and avoid my responsibilities as a Healer. There is only one thing that might work."

Mistress waited.

"I think Tol-mec must stay here, and Cloudheart must become hers," my voice broke, but I forced myself to continue. "My punishment will be this; I will not call him to me, feed him, or even pet him."

When I thought of never petting him again, such an intense pain struck my heart, I felt a knife thrust inside me. I struggled to continue, saying, "If Cloudheart comes to me, I will return him to Tol Mec gently and with great love. A broken heart will be my punishment. Will that serve, Mistress?'

"Indeed," she said, and this time I was sure she wore a smile. At that moment, I saw Mistress in her element, all gravitas and wisdom. She'd led us through the epidemic. She had made better Healers, Empaths and Priestesses—better women of us all.

A few days later, the last child who had contracted the Rhia sickness left Maidenstone alive in the arms of his parents. We all cheered. There were tears in many eyes as we waved farewell to the child's family. We clapped and clapped until they reached the bottom of the hundred steps. We shared smiles and hugs of pride.

Afterwards, Mistress Falcon and Ann Mali took me to the highest keep in the white tower. There they awarded me the Vermillion Cord of the Healer. I stood tall before them, filled with pride.

Two of the skills Mistress said I would need for my mission were mine. The final talent Mistress mentioned when I came to Maidenstone was the role of the Priestess and Far Seer. I was ready to begin.

## Chapter 15 – The Temple of Light
## The Hunger Moon, 2nd Month

The Hunger Moon began before Mistress asked to see me. I had been so busy with patients in the city; I hadn't found the time to ask about the final phase of my schooling. A young woman, tall and thin with skin the color of black coffee, stood beside Mistress Falcon's desk.

"Sab-ra, I want you to meet the Priestess Te Ran."

I didn't have to ask Mistress about the Far Seeing. It was starting. A fizz of excitement made my belly twitch, and I bowed my head in acknowledgement of the Priestess. All people venerated such women because they gave up their own lives to serve the Goddess.

"You have learned nothing of Priestess craft and Te Ran is the only person here who speaks the Kosi language. You will begin working with her tomorrow."

"Grandfather insisted I could not train as a Priestess," I reminded Mistress, recalling the gravity in his voice the day he said I was not destined for the Temple.

"I know his wishes. The role of the Priestess is distinct from the gifts of the Far-Seer. If Te Ran feels you have sufficient potential, you could learn to see the future."

I was intrigued. I wondered if Te Ran could open doors to my past, as well as the future. Could the Far-Seer skill tell me something about my mother?

Both Mistress and Ann Mali had known my mother. My Grandparents told me she had died at my birth. However, I always sensed some mystery they held back. She was the source of my deepest fears and fiercest needs.

"I welcome this opportunity, Priestess. Please tell me about the reading of the future." Excitement quivered in my belly, and a smile curled my mouth.

"It is called the Scry," she replied. "You begin by taking strong herbs which make you ill and disoriented. You will throw up. Once you pass through this stage, you feel distanced from your earthly life. You see and hear strange things. Most apprentices never get beyond this point. If this stage passes, you will see the future spread before you like the golden wheat fields of Talin."

I couldn't wait to learn what she would teach me.


The next morning, Te Ran was waiting for me in the flagstone entrance. We walked together down the cobblestone alleys to the Temple. The Priestess kept herself completely covered with white linen. I never saw her hair or her body. Only her feet were bare, save for a sole of leather she tied to her ankle. Her eyes were black, the color of boot polish. I had never seen anyone who looked like her.

I followed her into the Temple, around the center for worship and down the stairs into the lower rooms. These were the bedrooms for the Priestesses. Made of gray granite, they were small with a bed for each room but nothing else—no chest, no blanket, no pillow, only a mattress of sweet-smelling rushes covered by a white linen sheet. The rooms spoke of sacrifice and penance.

"These rooms are so cold," I blurted out.

"Cold, like snow is cold?" she asked, her face looking puzzled.

"No. They are so ugly." I shivered, thinking of the dedication of these women, knowing I did not want that life for myself.

"No, they aren't," Te Ran smiled. She lit a large candle. By the flickering light, I could see ancient markings on the walls.

I was amazed to see animals running, men chasing them, baby animals with their mothers, sunrises and storms of snow and wind. Her small chamber, which I found so confining, showed me a world outside of time. Already, I had totally misread. I quivered, sensing this might be the hardest training of all.

"How long have you been here, Te Ran?"

"Until I was five I lived with my own people. They are called the Travelers. Then the Kosi kidnapped my older sister, and she begged them to take me too. I lived with them and learned their language. They gave me to the Temple in honor of my Far Seer ability."

"When my schooling is complete, I will go back to my village in the mountains," I told her, feeling satisfaction in my chest. I had given my word I would never speak of my mission, so I didn't mention the fearful task that blocked my way.

"Will you?" Te Ran asked. "Many dangers line your path. I have seen them waiting."

Nothing about this morning was going the way I had hoped. I wanted to read the Priestess and instead she had read me. Frustration turned my mouth into a narrow line.

"We will talk of this another time, Sab-ra. You are here to learn the mysteries."

Now she was going to teach me the Priestess mysteries, something I feared and dreaded. I didn't want her world of contemplation and prayer.

"I want to learn how to see the future," I told her, biting my upper lip with my lower teeth. My shoulders tensed. I expected her to try to convince me how important the mysteries were, but again I had guessed wrong.

Te Ran spoke softly saying, "I can never return to my people."

Her loss struck my chest like a body blow.

Training with Te Ran was going to be like riding the White River on a barge. I would not be able to predict a single step. All I could do was hang on and try not to fall.

Te Ran handed me a candle, and we walked through a warren of rooms until we came to one with many shelves holding long, white hooded gowns. We searched until we found one that would fit me. There was a piece of silvery glass in the closet, larger than any I had seen before. In the light of the candle, I saw myself reflected, looking tall and serious. The hood of the robe covered most of my red curly hair, and my eyes appeared dark in the dimness.

Donning the robe had given me the appearance of a Priestess, but in my heart, I was not. I was an Empath. I was a Healer. I was a Banned spy. Even dressed in the Priestess robe, I seemed to wear the stolen garments of a stranger.

"What do you feel when you see yourself in the glass," Te Ran asked me.

"I feel repulsed by the dream of the Priestess and at the same time drawn to it, like the magnet cries for the embrace of metal."

"I see a time ahead when you will not reject this role."

"If I became a Priestess, would I have to stay here always?"

Te Ran nodded.

"I am sorry, Te Ran," I took a deep breath. "I cannot stay."

"In time you may change your mind. For now, however, I will teach you only the Rite of Supplication. Once you have learned the Service, we will start on the Far Seer training and the Kosi language."

"What is the purpose of the Rite of Supplication?"

"To help a worshipper petition the Goddess."

A warm satisfaction spread through me. I already had the skill to call the Wind Goddess. This was going to be easy after all.

The Rite of Supplication was a lovely ceremony. At the end of each service, when the musicians began to play, the Priestesses glided up the chancel nave holding tall white candles. A silver bowl filled with a clear liquid waited on the altar. A filament of golden oil rimmed the bowl.

The oldest Priestess tipped her candle to the rim first, lighting a quarter of the circle. Others followed. My task was to tip my candle into the center of the bowl and ignite a tall blue flame.

The day we began, I dropped my candle into the basin and splashed oil on the white samite gown of the head Priestess. Te Ran was furious and scolded me.

"Sab-ra, look what you did. Concentrate."

We started over again. As I tipped my candle down to the central wick, the rim flames leapt up and seared my hand. I shrieked in pain. Again, I dropped my candle. Te Ran grabbed me by my shoulder and marched me out of the Temple.

"Find a way to do this," she ordered. I had no idea how.

Over the next few weeks, I burned myself many times and had to still my skin to keep the pain at bay. I dropped candles repeatedly, desperately trying to avoid another burn. Once I even tripped the Head Priestess because my feet were in the wrong place. The training felt artificial and stylized. I never once felt the presence of the Wind Goddess in that Temple.

"Te Ran I am not a Priestess, I never will be," I cried out. Tears rose in my eyes. "I don't belong here."

"You aren't centering," she told me. "To succeed, you must concentrate on something beyond yourself."

111

Walking down to the Temple the next morning, I remembered how Maidenstone drew me in the night I walked into the Leopard's mouth. Te Ran wouldn't teach me the Far Seer skill unless I learned the Rite and I had failed. Perhaps the time had come for me to leave Maidenstone.

When I opened the door to the Temple, Te Ran stood waiting.

"Sab-ra, I see you are planning to leave Maidenstone."

I didn't respond. Jun taught us we must never read a person without their permission.

"I am your teacher here. I don't need your permission," she said.

The woman was infuriating.

"I have decided to give you a choice. I can tell Mistress Falcon you have failed to learn the Rite and return you to her, or I can give you one more chance."

Mistress might make me cut Conquin, or worse. The thought made me nauseous.

"Please, Te Ran, I would rather die."

"To stay here, you need to acknowledge I know more than you."

"You do," I told her, softly.

"Then, like the Novice you are, you will go into the Temple and stay all night on your knees. You will beg the Goddess for her forgiveness for your arrogance. When the night is over, you will come and beg my forgiveness also."

It was the longest night of my life. For most of it, I raged at the unfairness of the punishment, but when the sun rose and fell upon me, I wept. Te Ran was right. Maidenstone still had more to teach me. I wanted to be a Far Seer. I would try again.

The Wind Goddess lifted my curls in a caress as I walked down to the Temple the following morning. My breath made small mist clouds in the air. Once inside the Temple as the musicians began to play, I envisioned Yellowmane running in the golden fields of Talin. To my joy, I saw the fire spread perfectly across the surface, blue center flame joining the yellow rim fire. Even the oldest Priestess smiled.

For the first time in many weeks, contentment filled my heart. I had learned the Rite and Cloudheart had returned. Anticipation bubbled throughout my body. Confidence gave me a tall walk, shoulders back.


Later, we entered a room where bundles of herbs rested on shelves of wood. Te Ran reached for one bundle. I drew in my breath. The dried leaves were monkscaul, a deadly poison.

"No one can eat monkscaul, Te Ran. If burned, no one can breathe the fumes from the fire."

Te Ran frowned at me. "Do you think I need you to tell me of the dangers, Novice? I have been doing this since before you were born. Breathing the burning herb is necessary to enter the trance."

She set about making a fire in the black grate. The fire was burning well when she added a few dried Monkscaul leaves.

"Te Ran please stop," I cried reaching for her hands. "I have seen the poisoning of this drug. No one should breathe the vapor. Monkscaul can kill."

"Enough, Sab-ra. Do you need another night on your knees?"

I released her hands.

"The fumes open the gates of the mind to the divination. You will do this next," her face was like a blade.

I bit my lip, keeping back any further protest. She lowered her face to the fire and breathed in. She inhaled the smoke three or four times and fell back abruptly on the ground. Her body twitched. She drew her knees up to her belly and cried aloud. I knelt beside her, lifted her head and gave her a little water. When I stared into her eyes, I didn't see Te Ran. She had left the world.

She struggled to her feet, using me for support. Then I saw her rip in two. I shook like a howling storm coming down the mountain. I trembled all over and turned my face away, struggling to breathe, but my eyes kept returning to what was happening. One of Te Ran's selves stood beside me. Another watery image, not quite in focus, grew ever larger. The transparent persona grew immense, wavering in the air. Moments later, the trance state ended. The two images merged, and Te Ran was back in the Temple.

Relief flooded me until I remembered her saying I would have to inhale the drug. I had to find a way to avoid the horror. Te Ran stood quietly for a space of time as her glazed eyes came back into focus.

"Are we finished for today?" I asked. I was shuddering. My legs ached to run out of the terrifying Temple.

"No. You must breathe the fumes now."

My heart beat faster. I did not want this drug in my body.

"I beg you, Priestess. I have studied the art of meditation with Brother Jun. Perhaps I don't need the drug."

My body quivered like a small hulion chased by the mountain leopard. I feared the Monkscaul down to my bone marrow. The People killed predators using it. Those beasts died horrible deaths. I wanted the Far-Seer skill but dreaded the poisonous Monkscaul.

"You will do this," her voice was cold. She mercilessly forced me to a kneeling position. I struggled, but she pushed my face down to the fire and hit me on the back making me breathe in. I knew nothing except blackness. Dizziness spun me, and I left the world. I travelled the stars. I rode between the worlds.

## Chapter 16 – The Needle
## Vernal Moon, 3rd month

Deti brought me a note from the Temple a few days later. I took a quick inward breath, fearful Te Ran would force me to breathe the Monkscaul again, but her message told me to prepare for the Far-Seer journey. We would leave before dawn the next morning. A smile curved my lips and lifted my heart. I went down to the kitchen. Honus, Head Cook at Maidenstone, gave me leather packs filled with tsampa bread, goat cheese, bottles of water and dried sim fruits.

The sun was just rising as we walked down the winding path that led through shadows behind the kitchen garden. As we descended, ducked through the secret gate at the back of the barrier wall and climbed the trail upwards, my heart grew large. The first day of the Vernal Moon had begun. The wind gusted in small bursts. Spring rains would start soon. I could see the pregnant bellies of dark clouds.

"Goddess, thank you for this day," I murmured.

The mist that lay around Namché evaporated as we climbed. How I had missed the cool air of the mountains, like a drink of the purest essence. Above the pale white vapor, I could see forever. At Maidenstone, every color was indistinct. Breathing the clear air my mind opened as a bud becomes a flower.

"How long will be we climbing?" I asked Te Ran, skipping ahead of her.

"We will climb until we reach the Needle," she pointed to a sharp pinnacle. "At the Needle one sees beyond time."

"Why do we seek the future now?"

"Don't you feel it?" she asked, frowning.

At her words, the drumbeat, silent during the long cold days in the Temple, resurged.

"Yes, I do," I told her, my voice low with fear. "Something is coming that threatens Namché."

All afternoon we climbed until we reached a round valley just below the Needle. Te Ran vanished behind a boulder and drew out a black bundle.

"It is one of the dweli of my People," I cried happily, remembering my trip down to Maidenstone. I had kept intact the memory of those nights—nights we slept in black circular dweli on golden grasses beside huge warm boulders. I explored the cave and discovered fur rugs hidden in the cave's recesses.

"Look what I found, Te Ran. We can use these to cover the floor of the dweli."

All around me, early spring flowers opened their miniature cups. Delicate snowdrops emerged from frozen ground. Yellow winter aconite raised slender buds to reach the sun. I gathered tiny flowers and scented herbs from this land of color. The perfume of the laelia flower, the hallmark of the Wind Goddess, graced the air. I remembered baby Lia and asked the Wind Goddess to bless her.

When Te Ran said we would be sleeping in the mountains, a thrill flared through my body. Above us, a broad melting snowfield tilted high against the crimson sky of twilight.

When night fell, I heard Te Ran sprinkle the monkscaul on the fire and her harsh breathing. She writhed on the ground and moaned. The wind was high and tiny snowbirds rode the thermals.

"Come out here and breathe," she ordered. I didn't move. At last, Te Ran stumbled into the tent and fell asleep.

I walked outside and sat by the fire. Tiny wisps of gray smoke rose from the smoldering monkscaul bundle. They smelled like pepper. I wanted to be a Far Seer and I knew I might fail if I didn't inhale the drug. Fighting my fears, I knelt and took in a single breath.

This time, the drug made me feel feverish and energized. I could not sit down. I paced in a wide circle around our camp. As I reached the edge of a sharp precipice, I heard a sound from a crevice below me. I lowered my gaze and saw an Angelion—the mystical mooncat of the high range. The sound had come from her.

She stood on a rocky ledge, looking up at me. The creature's face was a white triangle with pricked ears and lovely eyes. She was much larger than the spotted Tar leopard that hunts in the mountains and her tail was nearly as long as her body. Pale strands stood in a wispy mane around her neck. I felt an urgent, undeniable pull to be with her, to touch her, to join her in her ranging up the mountain.

"Come to me," I whispered, begging. I wanted her so desperately; I almost leapt from the mountain to the ledge.

She climbed up the sheer rock face, her tail stretched out behind her in the wind. When she reached the campfire, I saw she carried an arrow in her mouth.

"Did you bring me a gift?" I asked. The arrow was longer than any I had ever seen. The arrowhead was red stone. The tip was fletched with white feathers.

The Angelion was enormous. Her eyes were level with mine. She made a soft rumbling sound, like a giant purring cat. I gently took the arrow from her mouth.

"Thank you, Great Mooncat of the high range," I said and bowed my head.

She walked to the embers and lay down, making a soft white wall between the smoldering monkscaul and me.

I felt the gentle breeze of the Wind Goddess and knew the Angelion had come to protect me.

"Don't leave me," I whispered softly, already feeling the desolation of her absence. "Please don't leave." I sat by the fire for hours, watching the Angelion sleep.

Much later, Te Ran shook my shoulder. I woke up, startled to find myself outdoors.

"What are you doing out here, Sab-ra, you must be frozen," she pulled me to my feet. "What are you holding in your hands?" she asked.

"An arrow," I told her. "A mooncat brought it to me."

"That isn't an arrow," Te Ran frowned.

I looked down. I was holding the branch of a tree. Te Ran seemed both irked and befuddled.

"And there are no such things as Angelions." She took my hand and walked me back into the tent. I turned my head back over my shoulder. The Angelion was gone. I saw nothing but jiggling air. Despair made it hard to breathe.

It was near dawn when I woke again. Te Ran did not speak of finding me near the fire, and I wondered if the whole thing had been a dream. We dressed and wrapped fur capes around our shoulders. My teeth were chattering. Te Ran sang the fire into flames and heated some water. We made tea and ate the last of the cheese.

Climbing higher was tricky. We struggled to find our footing in the stillness, as the stars streamed above us. The air was so thin Te Ran coughed. At last, we reached a flat area with a table rock balanced on four stone legs. I wondered how men had carried the table stone up the mountain. Made of white camica, the surface was shiny and as long as Grandfather was tall.

Beneath the table was a small sheltered area. Te Ran drew out a silver bowl. Placing the bowl on the table, she poured water into it from a glass bottle. The sun was rising.

She tipped the bowl to catch its rays.

"Watch the water. Tell me what you see."

I saw nothing except the reflection of the rocks around us. Then the water dimpled. The movement became more agitated as Te Ran whispered her secret prayers. I could see nothing, but Te Ran's fears tore across my mind like a furry hulion running before the Tar. Swiftly the water cleared and lay completely flat.

"Look now," she whispered. Te Ran seemed to grow fainter. Then I saw her rip in two. One self stayed beside me, her hand on my shoulder. The other self ascended into the high air.

"Now, Sab-ra," her voice echoed against the rocks.

I focused desperately on the bowl. Nausea gripped my insides.

"Look deeper," she cried. "The Goddess commands."

I saw the water fold, making ridges and valleys. Walking through the valleys of liquid, I watched a million soldiers march. I heard the sounds of their boots as they hit the ground. They wore black uniforms, caps with golden triangles and carried deadly silver weapons. One man led the phalanx. His hair was the color of the yellow snow where the dogs relieve themselves. I saw Mistress Falcon. Her hair had turned white. The water cleared and the vision vanished.

The drumbeat in my head pounded faster, harder. The Bearer people told Mistress the Army had retreated, but they were wrong. The War God was coming to bury Namché. I could hardly catch my breath.

"Did you see it," asked Te Ran, "Did you see the soldiers?"

"Yes," my voice was a whisper. "What can we do?"

"Nothing. They are probably not coming to Namché."

"I saw them come, Te Ran."

"Tell me," she ordered.

"I saw them at the door to the House of Maidenstone. Mistress slammed and bolted the door to keep them out. I saw a tall man with yellow hair; his eyes were those of a serpent."

"Are you certain, Sab-ra? You saw soldiers in the city?"

I nodded, too consumed with dread to speak. All the way down the mountain, I called in my mind for the Angelion. Her voice still rang in my ears. I ached to feel her soft fur. I wanted her to carry me up the mountain, all the way to Talin and beyond, travelling to the stars where there were no Elders, no Kosi, no banishment, no soldiers and no wars.

But deep inside I knew. Even if I could compel the mooncat to return, I would not leave Namché now. I had to help Mistress and the Novices during the coming conflict. I felt Duty encircle my shoulders and welcomed the cloak she laid upon me.

"Te Ran, please stop. Last night, did you find me sleeping by the fire?"

"Yes." She frowned. "This is no time for trivialities, Sab-ra, we must reach Maidenstone."

"I saw an Angelion last night."

Te Ran shook her head and motioned for me to hurry. As I followed the Priestess down the mountain, Grandfather's words returned to me. On the trip to enter Maidenstone he told me, "Your mother loved the Angelion with a pure, fierce devotion, more deeply than she had ever loved before."

Now the mooncat had come to me.

## Chapter 17– The Novices Leave Namché

Our descent from the mountain was a tumbling, falling, fearsome thing. Twice I fell and scraped my knees. The blood came through my leggings. My knees were stiff and sore. By the time we reached the rear court of the House of Maidenstone, both of us were bruised and bloody. We ran down the hall to Mistress Falcon's room and found her on her knees in prayer. Te Ran told her of the soldiers and the coming war. I described the soldier with the yellow hair. Like the black mountain Tar that will kill people when the game is scarce, he was a predator. I felt a frantic need to protect Mistress and the Novices from him.

"Both of you go to the Infirmary to be cleaned and bandaged. I will inform the Headman of Namché. Sab-ra, after you have eaten, tell Conquin to pack her things. Swear her to secrecy about the Army."

Te Ran and I were amazed. As far as we knew, Mistress never left the House of Maidenstone. She had entered at the age of ten and was now forty. We peered out the windows as the forbidding woman gathered a leather cape around her shoulders and strode down the hundred steps.

Cleaned, bandaged and fed I went to my room to pack. Cloudheart was waiting outside my door. After Mistress agreed to my self-imposed punishment, I formally presented him to Tol Mec. However, Cloudheart insisted on his own schedule.

He spent his days with Tol Mec but at bedtime, he always appeared at my door. The first few times I carried him gently back to her with tears in my eyes, but my actions had no effect. He must have learned some secret route from my room to hers, because by the time I returned he was already panting and laughing outside my door. Mistress finally agreed to Cloudheart's schedule.

"Cloudheart may choose his own destiny," were her words.

I wondered when she would think I would be ready to choose mine.

"Cloudheart come here." I called. I picked him up, carried him through the House and out into the back garden. He jumped from my arms and rolled in the dirt. He always found the muddiest part of the garden for his dust baths.

"I wish you would not do that," I told him, frowning. He panted happily.

When the bell rang for everyone to be in bed, I was back in our room. Conquin opened the door and came in. She held out her hands to touch mine.

"There are rumors of terrible things happening. Please tell me what you know."

Knowing Conquin's skill at reading the images in the minds of others, I showed her the soldiers marching up from the southlands. I showed her the yellow-haired squadron leader. I told her about the black uniformed troops ascending the hundred steps like a thousand rats. Her eyes widened.

"Conquin, the city needs to prepare for an enemy attack."

We talked deep into the night and fell asleep holding hands across the small space between our beds. We were so close by then we dreamed each other's dreams. Cloudheart slept on the floor, his dreams filled with captured voles and other puppy triumphs. How I envied his innocence.

We rose before the morning bell and were in the dining hall early.

"Conquin," I whispered, "I forgot to tell you last night. Mistress wanted you to pack your things. I think she's going to send us home." My heart lifted at the thought of returning to Talin. The Elders could not send me away again if a war was coming.

"Would you be happy about that?" she asked.

"I would be thrilled." I was breathing fast, imagining my arrival. I envisioned presenting Cloudheart to my grandparents. I saw myself riding Yellowmane in Talin's golden fields. Perhaps, walking near the Green River, I would find a way to achieve an honorable justice for Hodi.

"I assume my parents and the King of the Twelve Valleys would want me back home, but I haven't learned enough to be a midwife to the women of Natil yet. I wish we could stay longer."

"Don't be silly. You are a fully Entitled Empath. People in Natil will be grateful for your skills. They certainly surpass mine."

"I suppose," but Conquin's face wore a frown.

"I am excited to return, but I will miss you terribly," I reached for her hand. She squeezed mine in return.

Mistress entered the dining room.

"Good morning, Novices. I have news I wish I didn't have to tell you. The Harn Army is preparing to attack Namché."

The Novices looked shocked, several turned to their friends, asking questions. With an abrupt hand gesture, Mistress Falcon hushed the buzz of conversation.

"Quiet, please. For your safety all of you who have families in the mountains must leave in the next few days."

"How will we get home?" Ange asked.

"One of the Wool Trains is nearly ready to leave. Three of you will go in the first caravan. The rest of you will wait for the next Wool Train. By the end of the week, all of you must be gone."

I remembered Grandfather's Wool Train and hoped he would be pleased to see me.

"Conquin, Perced and Ryle please pack your things. Jun will take you down into the city. Say your good-byes. You will leave at evening."

My mouth fell open. She had said three of them were going in the first caravan. Conquin was getting to leave but I wasn't? My belly tightened with resentment.

"There will be hard days ahead with much privation, want and pain. War brings great losses in its wake. Soldiers who long for battle suppress reality. War does not bring glory; war brings only death."

I had never seen war, but the pain of so many dying shook my soul. Mistress held out her arms. Her anguish and love fell upon us all like a torrent. I never knew how much we mattered to her and now we were leaving.

"I pronounce upon you the Travelers blessing." She touched the three Novices, Conquin, Perced and Ryle on their foreheads and chanted the songlike words. Then she handed each of us leather sheaths holding knives.

"These have poisoned tips," she said, "use them only to save your lives or those of your loved one."

Why had she not blessed me? Perhaps she was saving her blessing for the Novices leaving with the second Wool Train. She took my hand and led me away from the others.

"Sab-ra, I have decided you will not be going."

My heart clenched. Why was she doing this to me?

"I beg you please, Mistress, please let me go. The Elders need to know about the war."

She took in a deep breath. "I know this will be difficult for you, but I have made my decision. You may walk down into the city with the others, but you must return when the Wool Train leaves. Brother Jun will escort you."

"Please," I begged again, feeling my heart torn into shreds.

"I cannot. I made a promise many years ago to your Grandmother."

Was I supposed to be here forever? I nearly screamed in frustration.


The town was bustling with the arrival and departure of wool traders the evening the Novices left Namché. Even the Iron Horse was there, whistling and blowing steam in the air. It was a vast machine built to take our wool to other cities south of Namché.

Conquin, Perced, Ryle and I walked through tree-shaded streets crowded with peddlers selling salt, spices and beautiful fabrics. Street musicians played quietly.

"Blessings on you," the merchants called as we made our way to the Wool Pavilion.

Jun took my hand for just a moment. "Is this the way a banned spy returns to her home village?"

"I'm not going." I suppressed the rage building inside me, but Jun heard anger in my voice. "Mistress is honoring some ridiculous promise she gave to my Grandmother. I am surprised she allowed me to come to the city." Jun's eyebrows rose at the bitter note in my voice. "Since I have to stay, I want to see Conquin and the others leave safely."

"Is this your responsibility?" His gaze was warm.

"When I saw the Harn Army in the Scry, I had a premonition. The yellow-haired leader is a threat to all of us. We must all leave before the invasion."

We reached the Ghat corrals, and I scrutinized the Wool Caravans. Grandfather was not there, neither was Uncle Hent. Jun led a fat, smiling man over and introduced us. The driver's name was Enuth. He and Jun entered the Teahouse. Through the window, I could see Jun handing Enuth some silver parthats.

Anger flared again in my chest.

Mistress was struggling to pay for Maidenstone, yet she had enough silver parthats to ensure Conquin, Perced and Ryle would escape the city. Apparently, I wasn't worth her precious silver parthats.

Jun left us to go to the city stables. When he returned, he had Conquin's foal, her reward for passing the Empath test. I petted him and saw how young he was. I wondered if he could make this trip. His hooves were still soft. Conquin flushed with pleasure when she saw him.

"I have named him Shine," she told me.

He was a beautiful gleaming black but skittish and not old enough to ride. I turned my face away from her pleasure. I told myself to be glad she was getting to go home, but envy wracked my body. I didn't want her to see my disgruntled face.

"Good-bye my young students," Jun told us. "Go to the Teahouse and wait until Enuth comes for you. It has been my privilege to teach you. May the sun shine on us together in the days to come."

He strode quickly away, looking very handsome. He wore a curved sword in his belt. I heard him wondering if he should join the Resistance. Enuth came to walk us to his Caravan in late afternoon. How I longed to climb into his Wool Cart.

"May the Goddess bring us to each other soon," I told Conquin with tears in my voice.

"We will only see each other again if you survive your mission."

"You knew?"

"I have waited for you to tell me about this from the time we entered Maidenstone," her voice scolded softly.

"Conquin, I beg your forgiveness. I promised the Elders never to speak of my mission. How did you know?"

"Sab-ra, my friend, I took the mission from your mind as easily as picking a berry from the branch." She rolled her eyes, laughing at me for underestimating her.

A flood of remorse filled me. Of course, she knew. I should have realized her skills were more than equal to opening the small doors of my mind. Our eyes smiled at each other, remembering the many days of silence with Jun in the teaching room and our eventual success.

Running beside the carts as they rolled toward the Leopard Gate I called, "When the war is over, I will come to you." Dust rose around the wheels of the great wooden wagons, sparkling in the late afternoon sun.

"And I will wait for you in the Valley of the King." Conquin stood up in the bouncing wagon and put both her hands over her mouth. Her gesture said words could never convey how much she loved me. A fresh tinge of pain nearly stopped my breath. The cart and my only friend were leaving.

I turned to walk back to Maidenstone, feeling abandoned. Then my heart began to race. An omen of disaster loomed up before me, dark as a thunderhead. Something bad was about to happen to my friends. The wagons were required to stop at the Leopard's Gate for permission to leave the city. I had to get to them before they were beyond the wall. I raced for the guard station.

When I reached the edge of the moat beneath the bridge, I inched my way down the muddy banks and slipped into the cold water. Luckily, the water only reached my waist. I was able to walk across to a post supporting the arched bridge. The stones used to build the post stuck out at intervals. Using them as hand and foot holds, I climbed the bridge support and emerged dripping on the surface just ahead of a group of wagons. Crouched in the shadow of the tower, I was barely visible.

I waited until Conquin's wagon nearly passed me. The huge wooden wheels would crush me unless I was directly between them. Timing my jump, I grabbed the side by the axel, a skill I had perfected on the wool wagons in Talin.

I hauled myself up, slipped between the sideboards and dove surreptitiously under the tarp. I realized instantly something was wrong. I couldn't see any of the Novice's boots. Had I been mistaken about which wagon was Conquin's?

Perhaps Enuth had taken my friends up onto the driver's wooden platform. I strained to hear voices. Two men were talking. This wasn't right. Enuth had no other driver with him.

"When we get to the boulders at the base of the foothills, we will stop. We can signal the Novice wagon driver for help, telling him we have a broken wheel. When he bends over to look at it, I will hit him over the head with this heavy metal rod."

"Do you think they will pay a lot for them?"

"A thousand parthats. Maybe two thousand for the one going to the King's Valley."

These wretched bandits planned to sell Conquin. The gorge rose into my mouth, tasting bitter.

"Remember, we agreed the Novices would not be harmed," the man's voice cautioned his companion. "You keep talking about keeping those girls. It worries me."

"Yes, no family would pay for a Novice who was injured or raped. They are tempting though," the man chuckled.

I had to stop these ghastly devil-men.


Hours later, a giant shadow fell over the wagon. We were entering the Garden of the Gods.

I heard the creaking of the wooden struts, the men hauling on the reins and loud yells. They stopped beside a boulder. Its chill shadow fell on the wagon.

I lifted the canvas a little and peeked out. Seeing no one, I jumped down and darted behind one of the giant stones. Below us, lumbering up the Wool Road, I saw another wagon. That one had to be Conquin's. I started running down the road—fast as a mountain deer.

A man's voice yelled loudly behind me, "Who is that? Get your bow. Shoot her."

Terrified, I kept running toward Conquin's wagon. An arrow whirred by my head, then another. I zigzagged to evade the fusillade. Arrows flew past me and lodged in the ground. With enormous power, one arrow hit me in the back of my thigh. The force knocked me to the earth. Cold and dizzy, I stood up. I couldn't bend my leg. Enuth hauled on the reins, bringing the Ghat to a standstill a hundred paces away.

"Stop those men," I screamed, pointing. I turned around to see the men running back to their wagon. They whipped the Ghat mercilessly. Pain seared my leg. Looking over my shoulder, I saw feathers sticking out from the back of my thigh. The smell of blood brought Hodi back to me.

I forced myself to yell again for the Novice driver. Enuth got down from his driver's seat and started walking toward me.

"Hurry," I screamed. Out of breath with teeth chattering, I managed, "Those men …they were going to ransom the Novices. I had to warn …."

When I came to consciousness later, we were riding in the wagon. Conquin was bandaging my leg. She had tied a piece of fabric so tight, the band cut off the circulation.

"Too tight," I mumbled. "Loosen it."

"It needs to stay tight," I heard Conquin's voice from far away. Her face was blurry. "I had to tug the arrow out through the front of your leg. Blood spurted everywhere. Lie still or you might die from blood loss. We are going back to Namché."

By the time we reached the Leopard Gate, the sun had set. When I first came to Maidenstone, a Priestess was waiting for me. Now I saw her again. She stepped forward through the fog. She must have carried me up the hundred steps to Maidenstone because when I woke later, I was in the Infirmary. Ann Mali was cleaning my wound.

"Are they safe?" I asked. "Conquin and the others, are they safe?"

"Yes, Sab-ra. You are quite the hero today. We can't figure out how you knew about the plan in time to get into the bandits' wagon. Mistress wondered if perhaps you were trying to return to Talin," she lifted her eyes at me, questioningly.

I said nothing.

"We sent a member of the Resistance to ride in the Novice wagon," I heard her voice get very quiet. "He will take them all the way ….to…the…Green…River."

I remembered trailing my hands in the icy waters of the Green River. The sun was shining, and I was very small.

When I woke later, Conquin and the others were gone. My satisfaction at saving them was short-lived. I couldn't walk for weeks, and I saved only three of the Novices. Even if Mistress Falcon changed her mind about sending me home, I couldn't go. I could do nothing but lie there uselessly. I wept in frustration.

## Chapter 18 – Mistress gives Sab-ra a Test

By the end of the week, there were only six of us left at Maidenstone—Ange, Lanel, the orphan Deti, Tol Mec, Mistress and me. I wondered whether Te Ran and the other Priestesses had remained in Namché, but the Temple was part way down the mountain, and my leg was too sore to go that far. Misery lay in my chest, heavy as an anvil.

Mistress made strenuous efforts to get Ange and Lanel to safety, but no wool caravan would take them; their valley was too far east of the Wool Road. Deti had no parents. She would wait out the invasion with us, but Mistress located Tol Mec's parents in the Third Valley. She hoped we could obtain the services of a salt seller to take her up the mountain to Rahsin.

Kieta, one of Maidenstone's cooks, bade us farewell. Fearing for her family, she returned home. Honus chose to remain with us. Ann Mali went down into the city to help a woman in labor. She refused to take me. I was improving, but still had a hard time walking all the steps.

The Bearer People brought news the Army was only a handful of days away. My dreams were full of ropes, knives and hangings. I saw the sacred Skygrass Valley destroyed by fire and ice. I saw Talin's People vanishing into history. I saw soldiers swarm the rooftops of Maidenstone like dirty vermin. I dreaded having to go to sleep.

The Wind Goddess held her breath as we waited in the beautiful silent city for the holocaust to begin.

Two days later, Mistress Falcon sent me to talk with Gordo. If anyone knew a way to get Tol Mec to her village, Gordo would. Gordo's house was only a dozen steps below Maidenstone. I could go down and back easily.

Once Tol Mec left, I would be relieved to have another Novice safely out of Namché.

Gordo's wife, Ken-dra, answered the door and welcomed me. I held out my hands to her saying, "I am so sorry about Malau. I know she fought hard against the appalling Rhia sickness."

Grief had taken the sparkle from Ken-dra's eyes, but her long black hair shone and her cheeks were pink. She was grateful to have her other daughter and son alive. Many mothers in the city lost all their children. Ken-dra made tea, whisking the pale green liquid and pouring the tea into yellow translucent cups. Their house was warm with the sun coming through the windows. Gordo came in and joined us.

"Honorary Uncle Gordo, there is a Novice whose family lives in the valley of Rahsin. We want to get her there safely but don't know how to get her out of the city."

"I may be able to send her with Ten-Singh," Gordo's voice was thoughtful. "Or perhaps the Kosi could take her."

"I saw a Kosi Warrior lurking among the trees on my way down to your house."

"Yes, I have hired one of the Kosi." Gordo's voice was defensive. "My family needed the protection."

I shuddered involuntarily, remembering Hodi and his awful fate.

At my expression he added, "I have assigned the warrior to protect you whenever you come to my house. Ten-Singh from the Bearer people watches when any of the Novices are in the city."

My shoulders were high and hunched remembering Hodi's wretched fate. Trying to make my body relax, I brought my head up and shoulders down. I took a shaky breath. I had to trust Gordo's instincts.

"Why does this appalling Army want to conquer Namché?

"Our rich land is a prize to the conquerors," Gordo told me.

"I hate telling you this, Sab-ra, but they already know about the Skygrass Valley and the blue diamonds."

I could not speak. I bent my head down to my knees, trying to gain control. The news made me dizzy.

"Can't our soldiers keep the Army beyond the curtain wall?" My voice came out cracked and high.

"Our country doesn't have an army, Sab-ra. We have only the Resistance and a few of the Shunned Kosi who work for pay. After the Occupation, if the soldiers find a citizen with a weapon, they will face a firing squad. This is a brutal force."

I thought of the knife Mistress had given me and tightened my grip on it. Having the weapon gave me strength. I left Gordo's house weighed down with apprehension thinking of Harn Army planning to invade the high range.

Twilight began, and the sun slid rapidly down behind the mountains. I glanced behind me to see the Kosi, half-hidden among the trees. The man trailed me as the Tar trailed the Ghat. I sensed his violent nature just barely under control. The black Lakt sat in a deep well in my chest.

When I told Mistress that Gordo thought he could get Tol Mec to her people with either Ten-Singh or the Kosi as a guard, she told me I could go along. I didn't think I had heard correctly.

"What did you say?"

"I am sending you with Tol Mec," her voice was calm.

Fear tightened my chest. I had seen the war in horrific dreams. Then I wondered if she had changed her mind and meant I could go home.

"Do you mean I can go to Talin after I take Tol Mec to Rahsin?"

Quickly, before she could shake her head, I continued.

"Gordo told me the Army plans to locate the Skygrass Stone mine."

"The Elders need to know this," I felt a bright brush of hope flare across my face.

"Sab-ra, I told you before I was constrained by a promise. This trip will be a challenge, but I know you will return safely to Maidenstone."

My mouth tightened in rebellion. How could she make me get so close to Talin and then deny me even a visit? She was unjust. Her face was set like stone. I was furious, but Mistress never changed her mine once she made a decision. I had wanted all the Novices out of the city, I reminded myself. Having Tol Mec safe at home in the third valley would mean one less girl in harm's way.

Gordo came to Maidenstone early the next morning. As we were getting ready to leave, Mistress told me Cloudheart needed to stay with Tol Mec for the duration of the war.

I swallowed my protests, but she saw my angry face.

"I honored Cloudheart's wishes to split his time between you and Tol Mec when you both lived here, but now he must go with her. Sab-ra, promise me, you will return." Her voice wounded me with its weapon-like determination.

Taking a deep breath, I promised, but she had wrung my promise under duress. I could not even meet her eyes.

"Ten-Singh is waiting for you at the Tea House. Get Tol Mec and cover your hair with a scarf."

"What if we encounter the Army?"

"The Army is still several days south of the city. You are going north. You will be all right."

"What about my leg?" My voice was challenging and angry.

"He has a donkey, you can ride." She didn't even sound sympathetic.

Tol Mec and I walked slowly down into the city with patient little Cloudheart beside us.

The white fog reached up to the first landing on the hundred steps. I remembered the day I crept from the sentinel pine forest after making my promises to Hodi. The fog near the Green River was a veil of sadness. Warm blood seeped through the dressing on my leg. Nothing about this day felt right.

Ten-Singh had a wooden cart and a donkey. I was to pose as Ten-Singh's wife, Tol Mec as our daughter. I made a sling for Cloudheart, slipped him inside and climbed irritably into wagon. Tol Mec skipped happily ahead beside Ten-Singh. We reached the Leopard Gate by mid-morning. A guard on duty merely glanced at us.

"It is good you are taking your family out of Namché," he told Ten-Singh, "Another day or two and the Army will be here."

When we were out of sight of the curtain wall, I released Cloudheart and got down from the cart. I couldn't stand riding behind the donkey another minute. The swaying made me sick. After an hour's walk, we reached a grove of trees and hid the wooden wagon there.

Whenever he got too tired, Cloudheart stood up on his back legs beside the donkey, asking to ride in the donkey's packs. I had a lump in my throat every time. I could hardly look at his beautiful black eyes, knowing I would soon have to say good-bye, perhaps forever.

To my surprise, the walking helped my leg. The bleeding stopped. The stiffness and pain vanished. We kept a rapid pace through the foothills for another day until we reached the unending grasslands of the Kosi. Early spring had arrived on the earth and the air was warm as milk steaming from Ghat udders. At night, we stomped the grass flat, making a circle for our sleeping furs.

One evening I disturbed a flock of grasshoppers. Long as my forearm, their buzz was loud as giant bees. They formed a vee and streamed up into the sky, humming. When we lay down to sleep, the grass above us made a perfect green frame encircling the stars.

As we walked, I asked Tol Mec how she came to Namché. She had run away from her family over a year ago. Her people were Ghat tenders and lived very simply. A travelling salt trader wanted to buy her from her parents. Fearing he would sell her to bandits, she escaped through the forest and made her way down the mountain. Some charcoal burners took her in over the winter. In the spring, she continued south to Namché where she'd found Cloudheart running in the woods.

We reached the compound of the Ghat tenders in late afternoon. As soon as she caught a glimpse of us, Tol Mec's mother glanced up from her work and screamed—flapping her arms and shrieking her daughter's name. They hugged each other tightly, chattering like birds. The family had given up searching for her. They were sure the trader had captured her in the forest. While Tol Mec was away, the mother had given birth to another baby. Soon Tol Mec was holding the little one, soothing him with baby songs.

"Cloudheart is a sacred temple dog," I told Tol Mec's father using my severest tone. "Tol Mec earned him by keeping him safe from the cooking pots. She has a duty to protect him."

Tol Mec's father said he would help watch him, but I was uneasy. These people were so poor. Would Tol Mec be able to protect Cloudheart if her own family were starving?

"You have to keep Cloudheart safe, Tol Mec," I reminded her fiercely, looking deep inside her soul. "I know you love him, but I'm afraid he will try to follow us. He is your most important responsibility. If anything happened to him, I doubt Mistress would let you return to Maidenstone."

After giving the family some silver parthats and telling them to send Tol Mec back to Namché when the war was over, Ten-Singh and I departed. I turned back to see Cloudheart in Tol Mec's arms, and the tears cascaded down my cheeks.

Ten-Singh patted my shoulder, trying to console me. By the time I could see through my tears, early evening had arrived. The sky was cloudless, pink from the breath of the Wind Goddess.

I was only one-day's travel from Talin. If I went to the village, I could find out if Yellowmane was alive. The promise I made to Mistress could not hold me.


As we ate our breakfast of Ghat cheese the next morning, I told Ten-Singh how close we were. "If we went west from here, I could be in Talin before sunrise tomorrow."

"I thought you were banned."

"I was, but I am awfully worried about my pony. A Lakt attacked her on our trip to Namché. Grandfather and Uncle Hent took her back with them to Talin. I don't know if she lived."

"Mistress told me you gave your word."

"Please try to understand, Ten-Singh. Now that Cloudheart is gone, I have no animal in my life. When I am without an animal who loves me, my soul begins to shrivel. Will you take me there, please?"

"No, Sab-ra, I cannot. If Mistress found out, she would never trust me again. I would lose my position guarding Maidenstone. This is a bad idea. Mistress expects you to abide by your word." His voice rose in unhappiness.

"I know." Shame brought a blush to my face, but I could not give up the chance to know if Yellowmane survived.

Seeing my face, Ten-Singh sat down on the ground in a dejected slump.

"Ten-Singh, I must go," I told him quietly.

"I will wait here for one day before I start back for Namché. I shouldn't even wait that long," he shook his head ruefully. "Are you sure your leg can take this?"

I nodded.

"Then take the donkey. Greet your pony. Disturb nothing in the village. Depart empty handed before full light. And don't get caught."

I turned away, not wanting Ten-Singh to see my mouth curve in a smile. Mistress Falcon's prohibition blew away in the wind.

Night was nearly over by the time the donkey and I reached the rising road that led into the village of my childhood. I pulled off to the side of the trail and tied the donkey up to a shrub. I checked my dressing. My leg was stiff but there was no bleeding.

All the sounds of the village were silent, and I crept like the spy I was to the stable. I saw my house in deep blue shadow and thought of my Grandparents sleeping inside. I winced. Why hadn't they even tried to protest my banishment? A sudden whinny screamed in the air. It was the voice of Yellowmane. A burst of happiness roared inside me. My pony was alive.

I slid open the door to the stable and lit a tiny candle lamp. "Yellowmane, quiet," I told her, quickly subduing her greeting. Then I took her dear face in my hands. A great song of happiness welled up in me. I wanted to stay in Talin so badly. Maybe my Grandparents would allow me to remain.

Raising the candle in the air, I checked the rest of the stalls. Hodi's pony wasn't there. Uncle Hent found Sorrell after our ruined mission and brought her back to Talin just before I left for Maidenstone. Where was she now?

I heard the soft glide of the stable door and huddled down in Yellowmane's stall. My heart beat so fast I heard thumping in my ears. I doused the candle, hearing the tuneless whistle the child spies use. It was Chiyo's whistle.

"Who's there? Is somebody here?" His voice was high with stress.

"Chiyo," I stood up.

He came closer, holding a lantern. He opened Yellowmane's stall door. His lamp lit my face. His face was dark as the night swallow's wing; his slender body silhouetted against the soft gray dawn.

"It is you." Surprise raised his voice. "I can't believe it. How could you disobey the Elders and come here?" His voice was disapproving.

I could see a wash of pink sky through the open stable door.

"Where is Sorrell?" Anger burned my voice. "What happened to Hodi's pony?"

"The Kosi took her. We thought they came for her because you left Hodi on your mission," his eyes were disdainful slits.

"Chiyo, please listen for a moment. You know me. You have known me since we were babies. I tried as hard as I could to save Hodi. I loved Hodi right down to the tips of his toes. I did everything I could to bring him home."

"If they knew you came here without bringing our women, they would give you to the Kosi."

"I had an important message for the Elders," I told him through teeth clenched so hard my jaw ached, "but they will have to find out some other way."

A wild impulse picked me up and put me on Yellowmane's back. "Run!" I whispered, and she leapt forward.

Chiyo lurched to the side, dropping his lantern into the straw. I heard a crackle as the straw caught fire.

"Stop," Chiyo yelled.

"Tell the Elders the Banned spy spits on the High Rules. I would rather live with the Kosi than here," I yelled, gathering speed on Yellowmane.

"Fire," he screamed. "Fire." I saw all Talin's doors fly open.

The whole village poured from their homes and the People grabbed buckets. All my life, Grandfather had warned me about the dangers of fire. I slowed and then stopped my headlong flight. I could not leave. They didn't want me, but I couldn't forgive myself if fire took the village.

I tied Yellowmane near the donkey, pulled my headscarf over my head and joined the row of villagers passing buckets of water from hand to hand. In the intensity of fighting the blaze, the pall of smoke and the pale light, no one recognized me. Or perhaps I had become invisible to the People of Talin. There was no reason for me to stay.

By evening, I caught up with Ten-Singh. He had started back slowly. When he saw Yellowmane, his face showed dismay. Then he reached out to hug me, called me 'Young Idiot,' and clapped me on the back. Both of us felt a huge sense of relief.

Two nights later, I heard Cloudheart's bark. He darted into our camp, burrowed under my furs and fell into an exhausted slumber. I was immensely cheered. Mistress was right. Cloudheart knew his own destiny. He was destined to be with me.

The next day we met a peddler who agreed to take a message to Tol Mec, telling her Cloudheart was with us. He was going to Talin after he left Rahsin. My rage at Chiyo and the Elders was gone by then. Saving Skygrass was infinitely more important than my feelings of rejection. I gave the peddler the last of my silver parthats to tell my grandparents about the Army and its threat to the Skygrass Stone mine.

When I told Ten-Singh about the Kosi taking Sorrell and Chiyo saying the Kosi might come for me, his face darkened. He knew the Kosi often kidnapped young women.

We decided to travel by night and sleep by day. By moonlight the great grass plains which stretched for miles, rippled like silver ribbons in the high wind.

We saw no Kosi until we reached the narrow cleft between the grasslands and the hills. When we heard the sounds of running hoof beats, we hid among the trees and watched. Thirty Kosi rode single file with their spears held upright, rigid. The gazehounds followed in an enormous silent wave of white. It was a sight both magnificent and terrifying. We were too far away to see if the Kosi Wolf rode with them.

The following day, when the sun vanished behind the foothills, we saw the rising curtain wall around Namché. I donned my head covering and placed Cloudheart in his sling. We tied Yellowmane to the back of the wagon. At the wall, the guard told Ten-Singh the Army had already occupied the city. He said we would not be safe if we entered.

Ten-Singh and I pretended to agree with him and waited until the guards changed. When the only illumination came from the enormous metal lanterns with their amber cones of light, we slipped into the city, silent as leopards on the hunt.

## Chapter 19 – The Captured City
## The Waking Moon, 4th month

In the days Ten-Singh and I had been away, a trickle of uniformed soldiers and then hundreds of troops had poured into Namché—like rats to a feast of the dying. Although I'd seen them in the Scry, their numbers shocked me. The Occupation had desecrated our beautiful city. Armed soldiers guarded every shop. Broken signs, shattered windows and garbage fires dotted the streets like piles of dung. The smoke added to the usual mist that lay over Namché making everything hard to see. Few citizens walked the once beautiful tree-lined streets. The Army had barricaded or destroyed most of the stores. One soldier marched a wool trader into the Garrison; his hands tied behind his back. The stink of death was everywhere. Walking along the main street leading to the hundred steps of Maidenstone made me weep.

One old woman stopped to ask whether we had any food or silver parthats. She told us when the horde broke through the gates to the city that the Headman of Namché came out with hands held high. The soldiers put him in the dungeon. He was old and almost blind. He did not understand what had happened. After his capture, someone smuggled a knife into his cell. When the guards discovered the tiny blade, they hanged him. I felt sick with despair.

We took Yellowmane to the city stables. Ten-Singh agreed to exercise and curry her each day.

Afterwards, he walked with me up the hundred steps to the front door of Maidenstone with little Cloudheart panting hard beside me. A Kosi Warrior stood just outside the door.

He smelled bad, and my nostrils lifted. He asked my name and consulted a list. He pulled the bell rope and Deti opened the door. I strode the stone corridors with Cloudheart at my heels until I reached Mistress Falcon's office.

I knocked and opened the door. She rose like the bent branches of birch trees when they shake off winter's snow. The invasion must have affected her deeply, I hadn't noticed gray in her hair before I left, now I saw silver blended with the black. Her hands were cold on my shoulders, but she smiled.

"Sab-ra, I am delighted," her face relaxed. "Tell me about your trip and Tol Mec's family." Hearing Cloudheart's little claws, she glanced down and frowned. "You gave me your word you would leave him with Tol Mec," stress pitched her voice high.

"I did, Mistress, but he must have run away from her, because several nights later he found our camp. I think he knew he belonged at Maidenstone." I reached down to pet him, very grateful he chose me.

"He knew his destiny," her voice was quiet. "When I told you to take him, I wanted to see which of you he would choose," she smiled. "Come with me to the kitchen. We can have tea."

"You must have felt panic-stricken when the Army arrived."

"I was desperate to protect the Novices," Mistress Falcon tightened her hands into fists. "Although the soldiers were ordered to prevent anyone from coming inside, except for those on the list, some troops got into the House.

"I sent a message to Gordo. He assigned a Kosi & a Bearer to guard us. The wretched barbarians will take no more from this House," her eyes were razor-sharp.

The kitchen was deserted. The hearth had only ashes. The black soup pot hung empty in the cold air. Cloudheart seemed disconcerted to see his favorite place with no scent of food or the cooks.

Only Deti, the last Novice, followed us. She made tea in total silence, and I gave her a compassionate glance knowing how difficult a vow of silence could be.

"Have you had any news of Ann Mali or Kieta?"

"Nothing. Some of the monks are still here, although most have left to return to their valleys. Jun is still here," her voice came down in pitch. The tea, my return and the warm kitchen had lessened her stress.

"I want to see him soon, but what did you mean by saying, *they will take no more from this House*." Dread came down on me, and my heart skipped a beat. "Where are Ange and Lanel?"

"In the Army Garrison with Captain Grieg." Her voice was sad as the grave.

I had failed. Two of the Novices had fallen prey to the yellow-haired vermin. I bent my head down to stop the room from swirling.

"I ran after the soldiers, beating on their backs, screaming. Sab-ra, they laughed at me." She was furious at their lack of respect. "They laughed at the Mistress of Maidenstone as they dragged my Novices away. They said I could buy them back with Skygrass Stones or gold."

"Goddess protect them," I murmured, feeling an awful pain in my chest.

Darkness descended on my soul. I knew in order to bring any peace of mind to Mistress; I would have to rescue Ange and Lanel. We didn't talk any more. I wanted only to sleep, to avoid for a short time the horror of their abduction. Deti had prepared my room. In spite of my wretchedness, there was pleasure in seeing clean white sheets and the view from the window. Cloudheart was sound asleep on my coverlet.

I lay awake most of the night, seeing Ange and Lanel's mouths screaming in terror while the soldiers dragged them down the hundred steps. I saw them clinging to each other, begging the soldiers to release them. Guilt laid her heavy hand on me.

At last, I could stay in bed no longer. Sleep would not come. I rose in the still dark house, crept down to the cold kitchen and sat at the table by the window until the sun flooded the space. In the quiet hours before dawn, I made a plan. I would use the Captain's desire for Skygrass Stones against him. I would trade him a counterfeit map to the Skygrass Valley for Ange and Lanel.

Mistress Falcon entered the kitchen early. I had already filled the stove with wood. The burners glowed, and the water pot bubbled. The scent of the fruit used for sweetening tea warmed the space. Mistress sat down and looked pensively out the window. Then she turned her eyes to me. Her gaze seemed to search my soul. Her deft assessment felt as if she touched inside my brain with her cool fingers.

"Are you ready at last?" she asked me.

"I am." A sense of quiet commitment filled my heart. This was not like the arrogance I felt when I escaped the cell, or the pride I experienced when I conquered the Empath skill or earned the Healer's Cord. I had no certainty I would succeed. I knew I could die. The lives of my friends were more important. Duty's beautiful gray eyes and pensive face smiled down on me.

"After the Novices were taken, the Captain of the Garrison came here. He offered to exchange the girls for a hundred parthats of gold, but the monks melted down all the golden coins we had. You saw Maidenstone's treasure when you entered the green tower. However, after Brother Nierta found the gold originally and tried to enlist Umbra, no more was ever found."

We were both quiet then, the room filled with our thoughts.

"I thought about this all night, Mistress. I want to give the Captain a map to the Skygrass Valley in exchange for Ange and Lanel."

Developing this plan had settled my mind.

Mistress Falcon gave a short horrified cry.

"Mistress, you should know I would never give him a real map. Do you think I could convince him to release Ange and Lanel in return for a false map?"

"It is an idea," her words were slow. "It might work."

"Grandfather took me to an old silver mine once when I was a child. I might be able to draw a map to the quarry. There was no silver left and the Skygrass Stones are found only in our sacred valley, but I don't think soldiers could know that."

"How long would it take for the soldiers to go to the old silver mine and return?" Mistress asked.

"It's about a week's trip, I think."

"Don't underestimate the Captain, Sab-ra," Mistress Falcon's voice was resonant. "I would take my own life if you were to fall into his hands. I think about Ange and Lanel every day and pray for their safety."

"Mistress, you must not even think of taking your own life. Deti needs you. Maidenstone needs you. I need you." I saw her lips soften a little, and her tense body relax against her chair. "I believe the Wind Goddess guides me to rescue them."

"Why do you think this, Sab-ra?"

"It is always the scent of the laelia flower that tells me she is nearby. Last night I opened my window to see the stars. The perfume of the laelia was almost tangible, like a gentle touch."

Mistress held my eyes and sighed deeply. "If you must go to the Garrison, Gordo will need to go with you. I hope you can get inside to see the girls. I have gone to the Captain's office twice, but I have never been in their room."

Her desolation waved coldly over me, dark as winter waters under banks of snow.

"Please don't despair, Mistress. I am with you now."

"If you are determined to do this, take your knife. Never forget the virulence of the poison on its blade. If the Captain or any of his soldiers lays a hand on you, stick the knife into their bellies."

That night I worked a long time with a knife and tree bark, etching a map to the old silver mine. When I finally fell asleep, I dreamed of Angelion. We walked down the hundred steps together. She was so tall that we walked shoulder to shoulder.

## Chapter 20 – A Bargain for Ange

Mistress Falcon suggested I wear the plain black robe of a nun, the garment worn at the final stage of Priestess training, for the visit to the Garrison. I tied a black scarf over my hair. When I was dressed, I asked Mistress for her blessing. Her whispered words lifted my spirits.

Gordo and I walked the hundred steps slowly. It was spring in the occupied city. Pale green leaves cast filigreed shadows on the stone streets of Namché. I keenly felt the contrast between the waking earth and the death-dealing invasion. Gordo and I walked side by side and I remembered Hodi and the days we trained in fields of gold.

A handsome dark-haired soldier showed us into the Captain's Office. He smiled warmly at me. The Office was furnished with a large desk and a chair. Black and red flags hung on the opposite wall. When Captain Grieg entered the room, I knew him instantly. He was the man from the Scry.

The dark feather of Destiny stroked my mind, soft as a drumbeat. Lust for the Skygrass Stones had eaten this man's soul. Even without touching him, I sensed implacable will and obsession. He would stop at nothing to find and conquer the peaceful Valley of Skygrass. If he succeeded, hideous machines would gouge the blue gems from our sacred space. Skygrass would become an open pit of death. I cringed and closed my eyes to destroy the dreadful image.

The Captain greeted Gordo pleasantly but beneath their words, their body language resembled a pair of rutting male elk, just before a battle to the death. Grieg spoke a language I did not understand, but the young soldier who stood with him rendered the Captain's words into the People's language.

"Good morning," the Translator began pleasantly.

"We received a message yesterday saying you have something you are willing to trade with the Captain."

"I have a map, but before I show the Captain, I wish to see Ange and Lanel, the Novices."

I reached inside the pocket of my robe and gingerly touched the handle of my knife. I knew if the Captain had me searched, he would surely hang me. I called upon the Goddess within to slow my breathing. I crept carefully into Captain Grieg's mind and saw the girls. They lay on cots, looking very weak. White-hot anger spilled from my heart and sped down my hand. How I wanted to stab this terrible man, this predator who ordered them taken to such a fate.

"Take me to them," I said softly, hearing a low vibration in my tone. It was as if Angelion had lent me her purring voice. The Translator started to tell Captain Grieg what I wanted, but Grieg nodded before my words ended. He could read me. Dread made me quiver.

The Translator and I walked down the hall until we came to a room locked from the outside. He said his name was Justyn and that he came from Tinsen, the tenth valley. He opened the door with a key.

I saw a young woman standing by the window. I almost didn't recognize Ange; she was so thin and wore clothing unsuitable for a Novice.

"Ange, I have come to help you," I could hardly meet her eyes. I was overwhelmed with pity for this beautiful young girl with no protection and no family, held hostage in this terrible place. She had bruises on her face. She gestured at Lanel who lay unmoving on a cot. Lanel slowly turned her head in my direction. Her eyes were open, but she did not speak. She was a husk of her former laughing self.

I walked over to her bed, closing the door behind me. The Translator and Gordo waited in the hall.

Goddess, help me, I prayed. Their near-skeletal bodies, their deadened eyes, struck me like the cold winds riding the back of the Snow Goddess. I struggled for each breath, hearing rasping wheezes and feeling my chest constrict in pain.

I knelt by Lanel's bed and placed my hand on her forehead. "Goddess, please help Lanel grow strong in health," I petitioned. Ange knelt beside me, and we prayed silently for their deliverance. After some time, Justyn opened the door and gestured for me to follow him.

We re-entered the office of Captain Grieg.

"What do you have for me?" the Captain asked, using the Translator's voice.

"This," I drew from the pocket of my robe a small faceted piece of Skygrass Stone. Grandfather had given me the gem on the trip to Maidenstone.

He grabbed my hand, "Where did you get the blue diamond?"

"Give me the Novices, and I will tell you."

I was no longer in the grip of a heart-shuddering panic. Rage had steadied my mind. The world narrowed to a killing point, deep inside me. Grieg's body was tight with greed. He flexed his hands. I knew he wanted to imprison me. I could feel his need to torture me to get the mine's secret location. He controlled himself with extreme effort and gestured to Justyn to leave the room. Grieg fastened his gaze on me. We locked eyes. I let my loathing for him spill out of me and on him.

"Take off your scarf, your head covering."

I shook my head.

Grieg's hand shot forward. He dragged the scarf off my head, pulling out strands of hair. His eyes widened. Momentarily unguarded, his control slipped and I entered his mind. He thought I resembled the women of his people. I shook my head, burning his eyes with my rage.

"I am nothing like you or your people," my voice filled with disgust. "I am a woman of honor and courage. No one who would steal a Novice from the Lamasery is like me."

The Captain bent his arm suddenly across his chest, as if he would strike me. I could feel how much he wanted to lock me in with Ange and Lanel. Frantic to distract him, I pulled the bark map from my pocket. His snake eyes fastened on it. Justyn opened the door to the Captain's Office. He had Ange with him. I reached out for her hand. When Justyn saw my hair, his eyes widened in pleasure.

The Captain seized the map. Then he lifted his eyes to mine. There was passion there, bright as fire mixed with rage. His eyes froze me to the spot, as the viper holds his prey in flesh-lock.

"This is not a map to the blue diamond mine," his voice was low and threatening. The tension in the room chilled the air. I took a deep breath and drew myself up as tall as possible. I told myself he would not kill me. He knew I had a blue diamond. He wanted to know the source of the stone. Justyn stopped translating. He could tell I understood the Captain.

"There is an old silver mine there, but below the silver there are blue diamonds," I told him.

"You lie. Tell me where the real mine is, or I will have your tortured." Grieg's eyes flickered cold as those of a large triangle-headed snake I saw in the market one day. I didn't answer.

"Unless you tell me what I want to know, I will strip your clothes from you and hang you from your hair. All the soldiers will see you naked. We will pour icy water on you, and you will die."

Rage ignited me; I became a flaming vessel.

"If you try to kill a Novice of Maidenstone, I will curse you with a snake that will crawl into your bed at night and bite you," I told him.

"Poison will drip from your skin. When you try to piss, only black blood will come."

I concentrated on the very tip of my knife and touched his mind. Grieg pulled back suddenly. Darkness came down into our souls.

"Do you think you could harm me?" his voice was contemptuous. "I would kill you where you stand before you could touch me."

"I have the Black Water poison and unless you set me free, I will curse you with it. You may kill me, but you will die the death where the pain never stops."

Suddenly, a whole company of soldiers entered the room. Gordo grabbed my arm. We ran from the office as if pursued by a wolf pack. I never let go of Ange's hand. Ange wept all the way to the hundred steps. When we reached the large door to Maidenstone, she dried her tears. A tremulous smile came across her face.

"You don't need to afraid any more," I told her. "The House is well guarded now. You will be safe, and I will bring Lanel back to Maidenstone, I promise."

As I said the words, a pang gripped my belly. I wanted desperately to rescue Lanel, but feared I had made a promise I could not keep.

I led Ange up the three floors to the Infirmary with Mistress Falcon following us. All the tiny vials and powders to treat Rhia stood on a high shelf at the end of the room, where Conquin left them when the Epidemic ended. Ange sank into bed, closing her eyes. Tears of relief rolled down her sunken cheeks. I examined her carefully and whispered to Mistress Falcon, "She is hungry, dirty and tired, but she will live. Tomorrow I will check her again."

"I am immensely pleased, Sab-ra," Mistress' eyes blessed me with her gratitude. "Do you think you can free Lanel?"

"I hope so," I told her, but the shadows of Lakt, the harbingers of dread, waited at the borders of my mind. If I failed, they would rejoice. The burden of Lanel, so fragile, consumed my hopes.

"Do not despair, Sab-ra, in this great task you have already succeeded," her smile warmed me like the sun.

Trailing behind her, down the stairs and through the corridors of the great house, happiness suffused my whole body. I recalled one particularly frustrating day during Empath training when I was trying to block my thoughts from the monks. Brother Marzun kept telling me to create a wall in my mind. Whenever I tried, he erased it, shaking his head at my puny efforts. I went to see Mistress and poured out all my aggravation. The words she told me then returned.

"I know you don't believe me, Sab-ra, but the day will come when you will long for the comfort and calm of Maidenstone."

I never thought I would feel the pride that wrapped me the day of Ange's rescue. I succeeded, I told myself. I saved Ange. Although I had failed to save Hodi, I had saved Ange. Mistress Falcon's approval gave my soul wings.

In my room that evening, I opened the long window and climbed up on its wide sill. I pulled Cloudheart up beside me. Together we gazed down on the city. A cool wind was blowing. Like a black star, the Garrison drew my eyes and thoughts.

"Goddess of the Winds, send my hopes to Lanel," I prayed, knowing how desolate she would feel without Ange. I knew the Captain's greed would drive him to the old silver mine, even though he doubted it would lead to the blue diamonds. Once he knew the mine was derelict, he would know I misled him. My days in Namché were numbered. My life was forfeit to his power from the moment I left the Garrison.

The drumbeat in my mind grew louder than ever. A headache so piercing that my color vision disappeared, hit behind my eyes. I saw the world in black and white. I had to make the rescue attempt before Grieg found out the map was false. I had to act quickly. Lanel might not live through the week, and if the drumbeat didn't cease soon, I feared I would go blind.

# Chapter 21– Sab-ra Oversteps

Deep in thought about Lanel's rescue, I recalled Gordo saying the Kosi who guarded the House was a member of the Resistance. I wasn't sure I could speak to a Warrior of the hated Kosi tribe, but I had a plan for Lanel's rescue. For my plan to succeed, I needed the help of the cook from Maidenstone and the Army Garrison.

The Kosi Warrior stood just inside the large main door. Memories of Hodi's horrible death nearly swamped me. I pushed my fears deep into my queasy belly.

"Hello," I began in my language and then, "Yahna." It was the word for hello in the Kosi language, one of the very few Te Ran had taught me before the invasion occurred.

He cocked his head to the side, interested.

"I am Sab-ra," I pointed to my chest. "What is your name?"

"Ghang," then in my language he asked, "What do you want?" His voice was gruff, and my fears of the Kosi resurged.

"Have you ever been inside the Army Garrison?"

He narrowed his gaze, nodding yes to my question. His dark eyes shone, attentive, acquisitive.

"I freed one of the Novices from the Army yesterday, but they still hold another."

He nodded and shrugged.

"It is wrong!" I burned with passion to free Lanel, still Grieg's prisoner. "The Novice is promised to the Goddess. I must free her."

"In war, men keep spoils," he shrugged.

This Kosi monster was unmoved by the bloody oppression of women. Wrath roared through me, but I needed the help of this barbarian. I drew myself up tall and sought control of my emotions.

"I want you to arrange for Honus to meet the Garrison cook. Do you know his name?"

"Day-toe," his voice growled. He held out his hand, and I took it. I read his frustration with his position, his rage at guarding a house of women and his wish to inflict pain. Beneath the violence, I could feel his greed. He pulled his hand away. An angry expression crossed his face. His intuition was minimal, but he knew I could read him from holding his hand. He didn't like it.

"How much?" he asked bluntly.

I was enraged he had demanded payment when he did not know everything he had to do. "Not yet. Not until you hear it all."

I saw his mouth open in protest, but my anger had grown larger than the entryway. For the first time, I experienced the fearful Rapture of Transformation. My body peeled apart. One clear replica of me stood beside Ghang. My second transparent self wavered in the air, growing larger. Neither self could control what was happening. I held out my arms for my other half, trembling, astonished, awed. I seemed to teeter at the edge of an immense abyss. From my vantage point, I could see the Kosi, small as a mouse. I had captured him. He was enmeshed.

"You will wait until I tell you everything you are to do. If you do my bidding well, I shall reward you. If you fail, I will curse you." My voice boomed across the canyon.

Abruptly, my two bodies merged and we were back in the dark stone entrance. Ghang stood as if rooted to the ground.

"You will take Honus to meet Day-toe," I told him, unflinchingly. Before all the mystery of the Priestess left me, I turned and sped down the corridor, vowing never to enter the Priestess state again.

Two evenings later, I went to the kitchen to visit Honus. I knew Ghang had already taken her to the Garrison to meet Day-toe.

The first part of the plan had gone well. Honus met Day-toe and learned Lanel had her evening meal in an outdoor pavilion. Day-toe thought he might be able leave the gate unlocked after he brought the food.

Mistress Falcon walked into the kitchen after dinner. Her voice was harsh.

"Sab-ra, you have overstepped."

Shame brought a crimson heat to my face.

"You should have brought the idea for Lanel's rescue to me before asking Ghang to go to the Garrison. You had absolutely no authority to do this," her eyes narrowed. She was as angry as I had ever seen her.

Turning to Honus, she modulated her voice. "I appreciate all of your efforts on behalf of Lanel, Honus, but I do not believe this plan will work."

Her cold eyes snapped back to mine saying, "I do not condone this." Silence conquered the kitchen. Neither Honus nor I had a word to say. I flushed red.

"I have been told the Captain of the Garrison is raging. He is furious to think a little slip of a Novice, dressed in the robe of a Priestess, outwitted him. Once he finds out the map to the silver mine is false, he will demand your death. Until the war is over, you will not leave Maidenstone again. Do you hear me, Sab-ra of Talin?"

I could not meet her eyes, but I nodded.

"I already met Day-toe, the Garrison cook, Mistress," Honus interjected quietly. "He told me Captain Grieg sent two soldiers to the silver mine, but they have not returned. No matter what you decide about Sab-ra, I want to help rescue Lanel."

Honus and I waited for Mistress' response. When she said nothing, Honus continued.

"The day after tomorrow is the eve of the Spring Festival. Day-toe told me the soldiers get extra wine and beer at the Festival. Many young women come to Army camps on such days, hoping to take the soldiers' money. Everyone will be distracted and perhaps we could rescue Lanel then."

"You have underestimated the Captain. The man cannot be tricked again. Furthermore, I will not give my permission for you or Sab-ra to make this attempt. It is far too risky. You could both be captured."

I dampened my pride and forced myself to ask, "Do you have an idea that might work, Mistress?"

"I have considered the Lethal Sleep poison."

It was as if Mistress turned into a stalking predator before my eyes. I vividly recalled my botched mission to the Kosi camp. I knew Lethal Sleep would kill a warrior. If tiny Lanel, not much bigger than a child took the poison, she would never survive.

"Mistress, Day-toe told me he brings Lanel's evening meal to an outdoor compound. Only one old man guards her."

"Could you get inside this compound?" Mistress asked.

"If I could take some of the wine from the Temple for Day-toe to give the guard, he would fall asleep. Then Day-toe would let me in and I could give the poison to Lanel."

"I will meditate and pray about this," Mistress abruptly left the kitchen, her Priestess robe swirling around her. Her footsteps rang on the stones. She was furious with both of us. Honus and I locked eyes. I took a quavering breath. Honus raised her eyebrows and let out a huge sigh.

"Gordo knows a Wool Trader who plans to leave the city the day after we attempt to free Lanel," she whispered. "He will hide Day-toe overnight and take him to his village the next morning. This could still work, Sab-ra."

Mistress had obliterated my plan in an instant. Honus was wise enough to see a way we might still succeed. Mistress thought my arrogance had erased Lanel's chance for freedom. I wondered if she cared that I was willing to endanger my own life to save my friend.


Mistress and Honus departed for the Garrison on the eve of the Spring Festival without me. Standing on the forecourt, I could hear the military band tuning up and the cries of street vendors. I paced and raged across the landing at the top of the hundred stairs but forced myself to wait. Trapped at Maidenstone, I could succeed now only through their efforts.

It was very late when they returned and I learned what happened. When Mistress asked to see the Captain, she and Honus were kept waiting over an hour, fuming at the Captain's disrespect. Finally, Captain Grieg and Justyn entered the office. Honus said Mistress Falcon's body tensed and her eyes gleamed. Her voice was low and threatening. She could have been an ancient lion-killing courser, Honus told me.

"I bring you a message from the Great Beyond," Mistress declared balefully, her eyes snapping. "I am High Priestess of Maidenstone. The Goddess speaks through me. She calls for the life of the Novice, Lanel. By morning, her body will lie cold. You will release her corpse to the Temple. If you do not, I will curse you with a thousand slicing knives."

When Mistress finished speaking, Honus told me she saw a faint yellow fog rise inside the office. Inhaling the vapor turned Captain Grieg to stone. He fell back against the wall, unable to stop them from leaving.

"The paralysis won't last very long," Mistress whispered to Honus, as they walked quickly to the outdoor compound, "Here's the wine for Day-toe and the poison for Lanel."

Honus waited until the street was clear of soldiers. Ducking into corners, she located the gate to the wooden compound.

She could hear the old guard marching inside. Still she waited in shadow behind a scrim of bushes, hardly breathing. Day-toe approached the compound, holding Lanel by one elbow. She leaned against him, barely able to walk. Honus handed him the wine and they entered the enclosure.

About an hour later, Day-toe and the old guard began to sing a drunken song. When their voices faded, she heard the gate click open. She crept into the compound. Lanel was sitting on the grass. Day-toe stood near the gate, watching Honus with bright eyes. Honus darted over to Lanel.

"This is the Lethal Sleep poison," Honus whispered. "Take it, but not until dawn. Te Ran will come for you."

Lanel nodded and took the vial, slipping the tiny bottle under the belt to her dress.

"Not before dawn," Honus reiterated.

Lanel moved her lips silently to the words, repeating, "Not before dawn."

Honus left her sitting on the ground, fearful she might never see Lanel alive again. My heart trembled hearing this part of the tale. We had to give her the antidote within twenty-four hours, or Lanel would surely die.

Honus and Day-toe raced through the gate and down the darkened streets. Behind them, they heard the sounds of the roused Garrison. The paralysis had ended. The Captain was ordering his men to find Mistress and bring her to the Garrison.

"The Witch hangs," he screamed.

Honus and Day-toe darted from one shadowed corner to the next until they reached the Teahouse. The Trader was waiting. He nodded for Day-toe to come with him. Honus told me she became a moving shadow, slipping closer and closer to the bottom of the hundred steps.

I paced the forecourt in the dark. My stress level was so high I nearly blacked out.

When Honus reached the base of the stairs, she called up to me and I gasped in relief. When she got to the top, we grabbed each other and didn't let go.

Back in my room late that night, I sought Captain Grieg's mind, but by then he had grown wary of my probing. I found nothing but his eyes watching. Like a hunter, he waited for me to put a single foot wrong.

# Chapter 22 – The Lethal Sleep Poison

At dawn the next day, unearthly music rode the bright air rousing me from my bed. From the window, I saw a Priestess cortege assembling on the forecourt. Six Priestesses dressed in black robes, head coverings and masks that showed only their flaming eyes, waited for Te Ran to lead them down into the city. They carried whirling drums mounted at the end of short carved sticks. Dark beads tied to the strings swung in the air striking hide-covered drum skins, making a concussive sound to a mournful dirge for the dead. I thought all the Priestesses had left Namché before the Occupation. Te Ran must have recruited them for the rescue attempt.

I had hardly slept the whole night before. I was terrified Lanel had taken the Lethal Sleep poison the previous day. If so, the antidote would do nothing. I grabbed a black robe and slipped down the steps to join the cortege. Mistress Falcon's prohibition binding me to Maidenstone never entered my thoughts.

I feared the Garrison guards would not admit us, but the soldiers seemed stunned by the Priestesses and their death song. They stood in two lines creating an aisle for us. The whirling drums beat continually, in time with the drumbeat in my mind. The sound was compelling—throm, throm, throm.

Once inside the Captain's building, the Priestesses began the ululation. It was a frightening supernatural sound, as if they called to the corridors of the dead. Justyn opened the Captain's door. I slipped into an alcove in the hall, terrified he would see me.

Te Ran's voice was forceful, "I come for the dead Novice." She used her Priestess voice. Her words brooked no denial.

"The Novice lives," Justyn insisted.

I could hear his confusion.

"I brought her breakfast earlier. She was alive and well."

"She breathes no more. Her body lies cold." Te Ran's tone of voice was filled with disgust for what the Captain had done to Lanel.

I peeked out of the alcove and saw Justyn's baffled expression. Each Priestess turned her head abruptly and locked eyes with the woman opposite her. Looking back at the Captain, they spoke simultaneously saying, "We ....will... see ...her ...now." The low menacing voices, saying the same words in unison disconcerted both men.

The Captain murmured something to Justyn and re-entered his office. Justyn came pelting down the hall, brushing past me. He turned his key in the lock of Lanel's room and went inside. Suddenly, he came rushing back out and dashed into the Captain's Office. He shut the office door, but I could read his mind easily. He had found a dead girl where a living girl breathed only hours before.

Moments later, Justyn led the black-masked Priestesses to Lanel's room. They sang a funeral lament in synchrony to the throbbing of their hide drums. The cortege entered her room and soon re-emerged. Lanel's cold body lay on a stretcher.

As she passed by me, still hidden in the alcove, I saw her white face and blue eyelids. The ululation began again. The sound held the soldiers in flesh-lock. We walked from the Garrison with death songs trailing in the bright air behind us. When I passed Justyn, he grabbed the sleeve of my robe.

"You may call on me for help," he whispered.

I almost screamed. I raced away from him. I was desperate to get back to my room, take off the robe and hide. I ran all the way up the stairs to the forecourt, passing six Priestesses.

I pulled open the main door, climbed the stairs and darted down the hall until I reached my door. I yanked it open. Mistress Falcon stood by my window. Her face was rigid with rage.

"I am locking you in," she declared, furious. "I can trust you no longer."


The next morning an entire company of soldiers broke into Maidenstone. I was in the Infirmary on the third floor when I heard the screams. I looked down from the window and saw them swarm into the house. They disappeared inside, but I could envision them looking into every room, gesturing with their long bayoneted guns. Then I heard soldiers lighting firesticks and the sound of them roaring into flame.

I darted over to the door and locked it securely. Ange was resting on one bed. Lanel lay sleeping in another. I stood with my back to the locked door. Fear made my heart race. I heard soldiers climbing the stairs. Then I heard the sound of something ramming against the door repeatedly. I jumped back and watched it splinter into a thousand pieces.

One soldier grabbed my arms, pulled them behind me and forced me to walk out of the Infirmary. The other soldier grabbed Ange. Lanel was still in the grip of the Lethal Sleep. I glanced back and saw a soldier prod her with his gun, but she didn't move. He thought her dead.

They propelled us down the three flights of stairs and outside to the forecourt. Smoke filled the novice towers, screams came from the kitchen. More soldiers pushed Honus ahead of them down the hall. One of them grabbed Deti who shrieked and ran. He caught her and threw her over his shoulder. She was grunting, hitting and screaming. The soldier set her on the ground and knocked her unconscious with the butt of his gun.

"Stop," I screamed. He backhanded me. I staggered and fell to the cool stones. Dizzily, I pulled myself upright again. The forecourt was spinning.

I lifted my eyes to the matrix of bright bridges.

More soldiers forced opened the door to the green bridge. When they realized the steps were made of glass and there were no railings, they hesitated. Then they began to cross very slowly. They opened the door into the green tower and disappeared. In moments they reappeared with Brothers Jun and Marzun. When the monks walked across the glass steps, they held their palms together in front of their chests. In seeming tranquility, they crossed the air canyons, descended the stairs and walked outside.

I looked up and saw Mistress Falcon in the highest room at the apex of the white tower. Her mouth was a silent scream of panic. I heard the sound of the soldiers breaking down the door. Smoke submerged the windows.

Several minutes later, coughing and cursing, the soldiers forced Mistress down the stairs to stand with us. They tied our arms with jute ropes and made us line up. My heart was beating so hard, I wheezed with every breath. One of the soldiers, squat and cruel looking, pointed his gun at me. He motioned for me to stand apart from the rest against a retaining wall.

Time slowed down …and down again…until each moment trembled like a drop of dew at the tip of a bright green fern.

I had brought this horror to Maidenstone by giving the Captain the false map. Facing what seemed the end of my life, I drew my courage like a shield around me. My eyes, ears and skin vanished. I could not hear, see or feel.

Everyone else stood at gunpoint, completely silent—dolls cut from paper. A soldier approached me with a rope, his eyes in a killing trance. He lowered a noose over my neck. A second soldier pierced my side with his bayonet. Warm blood dripped on my bare toes. Escape was hopeless. All I could do was take my mind away.

In my mind, I saw the mythic Skygrass valley and walked between its Gate Stones.


*The sun shone warm upon my shoulders.*
*Our ponies grazed on blue grasses.*
*The scent of the laelia rose to meet me.*
*Angelion floated down from the heights.*
*She came to me running, faster, faster.*
*I locked my eyes on Angelion's face.*
*In the darkness, I reached for the soft head of Angelion.*


The soldier pulled me to a standing position. He threw a rope over a gargoyle above the forecourt. He put a noose around my neck. I felt the rope tighten. The soldier carried a blindfold. He tied the cloth tightly around my eyes. I heard, "Ready…Aim…"

Then a different voice called, "Halt."

I heard harsh breathing and caught Mistress Falcon's distinctive scent. She pulled my blindfold down and started to untie my ropes. I was so deep in the Skygrass meditation; I didn't understand what she was doing.

"What happened?" I asked in a whispery voice.

"We have been saved," she said and pointed to a small man in a highly decorated uniform. Despite his short stature, he dominated the rest of the soldiers.

"Attention," the ranking officer called out crisply.

Every soldier stood at attention.

"Lower your weapons." The Army leader jutted his square jaw at the troops. They dropped their weapons to their sides.

"Right face. March."

The squad assembled four abreast. The head soldier followed as they descended the hundred steps. He turned back once and nodded to Mistress, as if to signify a promise kept.

I collapsed; a crumpled bed sheet, red with blood, lying upon the stones.

# Chapter 23 – Sab-ra is Discharged

Mistress lifted me to my feet, put her arm around my waist and walked me to the kitchen. Honus made her way to the kitchen as soon as the soldiers left. She was heating water for tea when we entered. For a while, we all sat there stunned and mute. Ange, Deti and the monks stepped quietly into the room. Honus graciously handed teacups to everyone. She might have been presiding over a tea party. The liquid was hot and sweet. While we drank, people began to talk quietly, still marked by the violence and our near escape.

"I knew Captain Grieg would retaliate against us for our trickery with Lanel," Mistress told the group. "Only the Commander of the Army could control him, which is why I asked him to come to Maidenstone. He reached the bottom of the hundred stairs only moments before the firing squad would have killed us all. We owe him our lives."

Slowly everyone drifted from the kitchen. Honus picked Deti up and carried her out of the room. She returned a little later, saying Deti was asleep before she placed her in her bed. It was one of the few rooms not set afire. Ange stood unsteadily, supporting herself by leaning against the counter until Brother Jun put his arm around her waist. He told us he would take her to the Infirmary and check to make sure Lanel was breathing. Brother Marzun blessed Mistress and departed.

When only Mistress, Honus and I remained, Mistress squared her shoulders. "While the Commander is in Namché you are safe, Sab-ra, but when he leaves the city, Captain Grieg will set his soldier dogs loose again," her voice was low with warning.

She was right. Each breath I took shrieked inside my lungs. The distant drum grew louder.

"You followed the Priestess cortege after I ordered you not to leave Maidenstone," her eyes were full of pain. "I told you once you were here on sufferance," her voice grew sternly determined. "I dismiss you now from Maidenstone. You are no longer a Novice."

Oh Goddess, no, I prayed. It was an appalling blow. My chest grew small and tight. The palms of my hands were slick. I felt beads of sweat on my forehead and pain stabbed my chest.

"We don't think you could stay here very long anyway, Little one," Honus' kind voice interjected. She had helped to free Lanel, asking nothing in return.

I struggled to find my voice. There was no appeal I could lodge. No protest I could make.

"Will Lanel live?" I whispered.

Mistress nodded.

"Go to the Infirmary and say your good-byes," Mistress commanded. "Bandage your side where the soldier's bayonet cut you."

During the Skygrass meditation, I had completely forgotten my injury. I climbed the three flights of stairs up to the Infirmary, holding my Novice gown against my side to stop the bleeding. Lanel was asleep. Her eyelids still looked blue, but she was breathing.

Ange lay drowsing, half-asleep.

"Jun," I whispered, "Is Lanel all right?"

"Somehow she survived." He looked amazed.

"Tell me what happened, will you?" I asked.

"It was all carefully planned by Mistress and Te Ran. Several days ago, Mistress sent me to the capitol with a letter to the Army Commander asking him to come to Maidenstone. By going to the Garrison the day of Lanel's rescue, you put the whole plan at risk. If Grieg had seen you, he would have executed you and Lanel before the Commander arrived," he shook his head in frustration.

Shame made my mouth quiver.

"Ann Mali was captured by the soldiers at the time of the Occupation and kept at the Garrison. She managed to escape during the arrival of the Priestess cortege, while everyone else was busy with Lanel."

I could not look at him, only at Lanel. More than anything, I wanted to go back in time, to erase my mistakes. Of its own will, my hand centered itself in the middle of Lanel's chest. She woke, sat up and recognized me.

"Lanel, I want to listen to your heart," she nodded and lay back on her bed. I lowered my ear to her breastbone. The beat was irregular and weak. Placing my hand on her heart, I prayed to the Goddess to let Lanel grow strong. I saw a lighted column in the air. It descended slowly to touch her body. I pulled my hand back and the column vanished, leaving only a vibration in the air. When I listened to her heart again, the beat was stronger. Jun gave me a faint smile and departed.

Exhaustion claimed me. I had never tried to heal with touch before. Slumped on the floor by Lanel's bed, I slept as if I would never wake. When my cramped legs and the pain from the bayonet wound opened my eyes, I noticed blood seeping through the bandage. I stood and got myself a new dressing. A sudden awareness took my mind. I had to see Te Ran before I left Maidenstone.

I walked to the Temple, holding the bandage tight against my side. I entered the complex of rooms where Te Ran and the others slept and called her name in a whisper. Instantly, I saw the curtain to her alcove shoved aside. She reached out her hand to me.

"I humbly beg your pardon, Te Ran. You and the others were magnificent. I failed to keep my word to Mistress. I have to leave now, because I disobeyed her."

Te Ran nodded.

"When I saw you in the cortege, I knew Mistress would send you away," Te Ran told me quietly. "Come with me. We need to petition the Goddess."

Together we walked into the place of worship, lit the candles and ignited the oil as best we could for the Rite of Supplication. No other Priestess was there.

"Where are the others?" I asked.

"They departed for home immediately after the rescue," her voice was calm, but a pang tugged at my heart, knowing she would never know her small nomadic home again.

"Te Ran, can you ask the Goddess if I will reach my destination in safety?"

"The Scry cannot be used to find a single person's future," her voice filled with sadness. "It is only for seeing events which will change the fates of many. However, I have an inkling your destiny may intersect with a larger one, so we will try. I inhaled monkscaul already."

Te Ran lifted the sacred bowl. She dipped a silver cup into the urn of water and poured the water into the bowl. She took me by the hand and we hurried outside.

"We must hurry. The sun is rising."

We each held a side of the bowl. Te Ran chanted quietly in the Kosi tongue, the language I never had time to learn. I'm going to fail, I thought. The dark Lakt watched me from their lairs in the high mountains of my soul. I lifted my eyes to the mountains standing proud against the sky and sought to focus. I saw nothing in the bowl except water and sky.

"Goddess, help me," I whispered.

Te Ran stopped chanting. "Did you see anything?"

"No," I murmured softly.

"I saw you on the mountain. You were with a Kosi Warrior. The image was blurred, but it seemed to me you stepped into his arms. He smiled down at you."

I frowned but was silent, hoping she would tell me more.

"Sab-ra, could you dedicate your life to serving the Goddess? If so, I could keep you here. However, taking vows as a Priestess means that you could never marry or have children," her face was unreadable, withdrawn.

"I must leave Maidenstone, Te Ran," my voice was sad. "The Priestess state terrifies me, and I do not believe my future lies in the Temple. Did you see anything else?" She shook her head, but I saw a tiny hesitation before she responded. Te Ran saw more in the Scry than she was willing to share.

"I sense the journey will be powerful for you, a trip with deep meaning. I will petition the Goddess for her protection."

We went inside and sat together in her small cell-like room. She had bread, cheese and one small piece of fruit. I refused to eat her food; she had so little. I told her about Captain Grieg's threat to tear the clothes from my body, hang me upside down by my hair and pour water on me until I died.

"I fear I will be captured trying to leave Namché. Would you cut my hair?"

"Yes. I will shave your head and give you a drug to darken the color of your eyes."

I hesitated at the thought of my long red hair gone but knew I had to be in disguise to get past Captain Grieg's soldiers. I knelt in front of the stone sink in her alcove and she poured warm water over my head.

When my hair was fully wet, Te Ran got a knife and used a whetstone to sharpen it. A breeze shivered across my scalp as the long hairs fell in a shining tangle to the gray stone floor of her cell. Te Ran darkened my eyebrows with kohl and put stinging drops in my eyes.

In the reflecting glass, I saw a bald young boy with eyes the color of wild blueberries.

"Farewell, Te Ran." My mouth tightened, trying to prevent my tears.

"Wait a moment, Sab-ra."

She reached into a cupboard and brought out the beautiful white on ivory braided Cords of the Priestess and Far-Seer.

"I could not see the future in the Scry bowl today, Te Ran. I don't deserve either Cord."

"You saw the Army coming when we went up the mountain. Therefore, you are Far-Seer. The Transformation has come to you once already. Therefore, I know you could become a Priestess. Even though you saw nothing today, you deserve both Cords."

I folded the Cords and put them in my pocket, unwilling to fasten them around my waist. "I will wear them when the time is right," I said, feeling a profound sense of appreciation for all she had given me.

"We may never see each other again," Te Ran said.

I bowed, knowing she had seen my future, although she kept the outcome from me. She bent her head and I kissed her coffee colored brow.

## Chapter 24 - Sab-ra Learns the Truth

When I reached the side door to Maidenstone, Ten-Singh stood at guard. I bade him a fond farewell and hurried to Mistress Falcon's office. I wanted to tell her my plan to escape from Namché. When I entered her office, I could tell at a glance, she had not forgiven me. Withdrawn and cold, I saw the Mistress Falcon I had known from the early days of training.

"Mistress Falcon," I bowed low.

She stood behind her desk, not speaking. Then with a little frown, she rose from her chair. "Goddess protect me, Sab-ra, I didn't recognize you."

"Mistress, I beg you to forgive me. My plan to rescue Lanel was born of desire, my own desire, to be important. I know now I would have failed. My heedlessness put all your work at risk."

There was a long silence. Mistress sighed. "I know you want to be a hero, Sab-ra," she told me quietly, her face etched in sadness, "but there is always a price to be paid for heroism. You did not die, as many heroes do, but you can no longer be an acolyte here. You must seek your destiny far from Maidenstone."

"I have no home but Maidenstone," I wailed. "I have no family. Only you." My lips trembled.

"Come and sit down, Sab-ra," she indicated a chair. "You gravely disappointed me by failing to keep your word to stay at Maidenstone when Te Ran went to the Garrison for Lanel, but as a sign of my gratitude for your help with Ange, I have decided to tell you about your mother."

I drew in a sharp breath.

"She was much like you, Sab-ra, brave, impetuous and proud. She came to Namché in search of her older brother."

"He was a man who yearned to see the wild animals of our land. He learned about the Angelion and the blue sheep called the Baral. Most did not believe these creatures existed. They thought them myths or animals which died out long ago."

I waited hardly breathing.

"When his family heard nothing from him for many months, your mother was sent to find him. She travelled here to the House of Maidenstone."

"Mistress, could you tell me her name?" My chest caught in a desperate ache, my life came from hers, but I knew nothing about her.

"Her name was Ashlin, Ashlin of Viridian. Your Grandfather, Silo'am, happened to be in Namché selling wool and gemstones at the time. Your mother approached his Wool Train and asked if he knew anything about her brother, Linc. He told her the Bearers had seen him in the mountains above Halfhigh."

I could see my mother's red curls as she made her way down the hundred steps toward the Wool Market. Entranced by the story of her life, my life, I lifted my eyes to Mistress begging for more.

"She engaged your Grandparents' son Dani to take her to the upper range where she hoped to find her brother."

"Was he there?" How I prayed she found him living.

"Sadly, she found only his body, lying just outside a cave. When your mother and Dani entered the cavern, they saw a female Angelion with a child. Both of them were thin, the baby nearly dead. The mother Angelion disappeared into the mountain when she heard their voices. Your uncle had given all his food to the mooncats. He died of starvation."

My heart ached, thinking of his courage and his sacrifice.

———

"Your parents camped for several months with the small one. They named him Sumulus. He grew strong and fat with their care."

"Was Dani my father? Is he alive?"

"Be patient, Sab-ra. Let me tell the story. During the time they cared for the young Angelion, your parents fell in love. At the end of the summer, they descended the mountain and reached Halfhigh. Sumulus was strong enough to survive on his own then. They bade him farewell and continued on to Talin. Several weeks later, your mother woke hearing Samulus call her. When the dreams came every night, she insisted they return to Halfhigh."

My mother had been unwavering in her commitment to the baby Angelion. Her feelings mirrored my own devotion to Yellowmane and Cloudheart. I smiled inwardly, knowing we were alike in our love for animals.

"The storms of autumn had begun. While on the trek, your father fell into an ice crevasse."

I took in a breath.

"He screamed your mother's name as he fell. She saw his broken body lying unmoving, far below. She tried to climb down to him but the walls of the crevasse were slick with ice. When she knew he was dead, she left for Talin. Your Grandmother discovered she was pregnant and sent her here for your delivery. You were born right here, Sab-ra, at Maidenstone House."

Born at Maidenstone. I was dumbfounded. A shiver raced through me. In my mind, I saw silver drapes billow before a great open window. Now I knew why Maidenstone had called to me as a mother called her child.

"You don't have to tell me the rest, Mistress. Grandmother told me my mother died giving birth to me. I don't need to hear that tale again."

"No, Sab-ra. It's what your Grandmother told you, but your mother left you here and returned to her own people."

The words seemed torn from her mouth.

"No," I cried, crossing my arms over my chest.

"Why would she abandon me?" I closed my eyes against the pain.

"Try to understand, Sab-ra. At the time you were born, Mongols from the north occupied the city. The soldiers ordered all white people out of Namché, but your mother was too pregnant to leave. You were a terribly weak infant. You couldn't even lift your head. No one thought you would live. She feared you would die on the long trail or in an Army prison."

My mother left me. Like Grandmother, my mother hadn't wanted me either.

Mistress bowed her head as if the heaviness of this information had weighed her down all these years.

"All I could do was to send a message to tell Ellani that her granddaughter waited for her. She came and took you to Talin."

I saw Mistress Falcon's compassion for my Grandmother shine on her face and understood the reasons for Grandmother's resentment of me. She must have been enraged when my mother left me behind.

"Just before Ashlin left," Mistress continued, "she told me she would return for you someday, if you lived. She promised me. I still believe she will."

I sought desperately for the maturity to understand the reasons she left me. My mother gave me up to save my life, I told myself fiercely. She loved me enough to give me life and then to save it.

"There is one more part to this tale, but I don't believe it is mine to tell you. Ask your Grandmother. When she is ready, she will give you the last of the story."

We sat silent a long time.

"Why didn't Grandmother tell me this?"

"You remember me saying I was constrained by a promise I gave your Grandmother?"

I nodded.

"She feared you would go in search of Sumulus too young and you would die in the high mountains, just as your father had."

Like a spark, the love of Mother and Grandmother, came together in me like the twining of a circle. For the first time I felt I had a family. A family flawed, with members missing, but a family nonetheless.

"Sab-ra, you are distinctive. Te Ran has seen you as Priestess. The demon monk spoke to you, as he does to all Mistresses of Maidenstone. Someday you might even take my place."


I slipped to the floor by Mistress Falcon's feet and laid my head on her knee with great shuddering sighs. I cried a long time, heaving dry sobs. Finally, I raised my head.

"Mistress, I cannot say how much this all means to me. I have waited for the truth so long," I took a calming breath. "May I tell you something now?"

Mistress nodded.

"All my life I have felt like an outcaste. Among the children of Talin, I was the only child who didn't have a mother or a father. I didn't look like any of the Talinese either. The other children avoided me. Grandfather was kind to me when I was a little girl, but when I started spy training, he pulled away."

Mistress nodded in understanding.

"No one except Hodi would train with me. After the failed mission, Talin cast me out. My Grandparents didn't even lodge a protest. They seemed glad to get rid of me," bitterness tasted like tannin in my mouth.

"I bonded so tightly to my pony, Yellowmane, because I was desperate for someone who would care for me. I cleaved to Conquin and then to Cloudheart because they gave me unconditional love, something I had never felt before."

Sharing this seemed to help. The pain in my chest began to ease.

"I sensed this, Sab-ra. I was incredibly frustrated when you escaped the cell. I could have wrung your neck when you crossed the green bridge into the monk's tower. Then I saw you growing and maturing during the epidemic. I know why you worked so hard." Her voice grew low and sweet. "It was to earn my love, wasn't it?"

"Yes, Mistress." I tried in vain to hold back the tears.

Her smile was rueful, as if she regretted so many days lost. "Why did you go to Talin after promising me you would not?"

"You knew?"

Mistress nodded.

"On the trip to begin my schooling at Maidenstone, a Lakt poisoned my pony. A Priestess treated her at the Leopard Gate. Grandfather took Yellowmane back to Talin, but I never knew whether she lived or died."

"I see."

"With both Cloudheart and Yellowmane gone," I paused. "It is difficult to describe, Mistress, I can only tell you it was as if I lost contact with my soul."

"It would have helped if you had shared the reason you wanted to go to Talin," Mistress put in dryly. "Now, tell me why you joined the Priestess cortege."

"It was because I promised Ange I would bring Lanel home. And for the smile."

"What do you mean—the smile?"

"To see the smile on your face the day I rescued Ange. The smile when you said, 'Do not despair, Sab-ra, in this great task you have already succeeded.' "

She reached for my hand. "It took us too long to appreciate each other."

"You said my mother wanted me to give Sumulus a message?"

"Yes. She wanted him to know she loved him and that she planned to return to him one day."

Mistress reached behind her desk and opened a drawer in the wall cupboard. She handed me a woven red-and-yellow blanket.

"This is the blanket your mother and Sumulus shared when they were together at Halfhigh. I hope it will lure Sumulus close enough that you can give him your mother's message."

A long ripple of relief ran through my body. I had wanted the truth about my parents my whole life and I was deeply grateful, but I understood that the cost of the story was leaving Maidenstone. Mistress and I touched the tips of fingers for just a moment.

I sang

*A vow of silence was required,*
*Songs of silence I have sung.*
*I leave you now to scale the mountain*

*All your praises I give tongue.*

She sang

*I promise you in the days to come,*
*When you ache to join me here,*
*I will wait for your return*
*Tho' the days be dark and sere.*


We held hands until I broke the contact and ran from her room, looking for all the world like a small boy in an ill-fitting uniform, with a cap and a shaved head.

## Chapter 25 - The Trip to Nowhere

I could not leave without saying a final good-bye to Honus. When I got to the kitchen, Cloudheart had a stolen carrot in his mouth. Whenever she tried to take it away, he mock growled and hid under a chair.

"Greetings, Honorary Grandmother," I smiled sadly. "I must leave you soon. Many years may pass before we see each other again."

Honus gave a cry of surprise, "Sab-ra?"

Grinning, I took off my cap, showing her my shaved head.

With tears in her eyes, she hugged me.

"Did you know I have been discharged?"

"It is because you went with the Priestess cortege to rescue Lanel?"

"Yes," my lips tightened, "And for many other mistakes. Could you make me enough food for a ten-day journey?"

I gazed at the walls of stone and the soot-darkened stove, which warmed this place on even the coldest winter mornings. I saw the kitchen garden, where the lime green leaves on berry bushes waved in the cool spring wind. I saw the pure soul of Honus and honored her courage in taking on the Lanel's rescue, the attempt I nearly ruined.

"I want to see Lanel and Ange before I leave."

"I'll come with you. I have their supper."

We walked the stairs carrying hot soup, bread and cheese. Ange came to the door and helped us with the food trays. Lanel raised herself up on one elbow but in her eyes, I saw the hopeless despair of the captive.

I took off my cap and swung around in a circle. "It is Sab-ra," I said, laughing. Ange covered her smile with her pillow.

"Are you well, Ange?"

"I am," Ange was still laughing at me.

Her joy made pleasure rise in me, warm as a summer afternoon.

"And you, Lanel?" She held out her hands to me, and I took them in mine. A storm of iron filings seared my heart. "Jun will come and take the pain away, my friend. You are free now, like the snow birds which fly with the winter wind."

"I cannot be here," she managed in a whisper. "I am unclean."

I looked down at her—in her clean white shift, between clean white sheets, on a clean white bed—and felt a pang of sympathy she would judge herself so harshly.

"This too will pass away. You will grow strong. In time, you will laugh in the kitchen with Kieta and Honus. For now, you must eat and sleep; mend and heal."

"Will you come and visit us each day?" Ange asked.

"No, dear friend, I am leaving Maidenstone soon," I turned my head quickly away before she saw the tears forming.

"Why, Sab-ra?" Ange's face wore two frown lines between her eyebrows.

I didn't want them to know Mistress dismissed me because I joined the Priestess cortege.

"Do you have to go because you rescued us?" Lanel's countenance had a guilty expression.

I sought control over my face. "Since the early days of Healer training, I have heard a drumbeat in my mind. I think the drum pounds to warn me about Captain Grieg. He said he would hang me naked from my hair. He seeks my death. I will only be safe in the high range."

"Do you want to leave?" Lanel asked.

"It's my only option," I told them. Ange nodded. Lanel seemed somewhat eased of guilt and pain. Her cheeks were pinker than before. The door to the Infirmary opened. To my delight, Ann Mali walked in.

"Mistress Healer," I ran over and hugged her. "I am so terribly pleased you are here."

"I will miss you, Sab-ra," her face filled with compassion. Sympathy showed in every dear wrinkle.

"And I will miss you. You taught me so much. We could never have saved the children during the Epidemic without your experience and knowledge. I will honor you the rest of my life."

I kissed both her rounded cheeks, smelling the sweet talc she wore. I wanted to stay longer, but the drumbeat in my mind beat louder each minute. I was running out of time.

The moon was a waning crescent, the night I left Maidenstone. A million stars filled the dark blue sky. The laelia flower opened, presenting us with her gift, a waving tendril of scent. Candle lamps from Maidenstone lit the secret path, which descended sharply down the back of the mesa.

Honus and I stood waiting in the kitchen garden for Ghang to return. Mistress had ordered him to be my bodyguard on the trip. In the stillness, we heard the distinctive clip-clop of horses' hooves. Ghang was leading three mounts up the path. He had purchased two horses and brought Yellowmane from the city stables. I was delighted to see her. Ten-Singh had cared for her well. She was solid, shiny and well muscled. She wore new horseshoes on her feet. We placed our food carefully in her saddlebags. I brought Cloudheart's sleeping sack so he could rest comfortably on the trail. Mistress came to say a last good-bye as we were loading the horses.

"Sab-ra, Ghang gets half his pay to take you into the mountains and a Skygrass Stone when he returns."

"Have your Grandmother tell him the last words she spoke when she left here with baby Dani. Once he brings these words to me, I will know you arrived safely."

"Mistress, I'm not sure I will even be allowed to enter Talin. Do you think I should go there?" My voice broke, husky with unshed tears.

"No. You must go to the Kosi," her face was calm and serene. "You will complete your mission. I have done what I could to ease your path. Ghang knows the location of their camps. Once you have succeeded, you can return to Talin. If Ghang fails to protect you, I will pour hot melted lead into his ear when he sleeps." She gave a sort of half grin. "I have no doubt he will guard you unceasingly."

I thought of the mission before me and shivered. I recalled Te Ran seeing me in the embrace of a Kosi warrior. Her fore reading troubled me deeply. It was more likely he had attacked me, I thought.

"One more thing," Mistress paused, "I must ask you to leave Cloudheart here."

I made a soft sad sound. The pain in my heart was fierce.

"Mistress Falcon, if I leave Cloudheart here, he will feel abandoned. You know I left my spy partner Hodi on our first mission. The Kosi Warriors killed him." A wave of remorse silenced my voice.

Mistress Falcon put her hand on my head and uttered the words I never thought to hear from this strong woman.

"Did you hear me, Sab-ra? I am *asking* you. Trust me when I tell you, Cloudheart will be safer here with us."

I bowed my head. Cloudheart was tearing around the stone stoop, tracking down some unsuspecting vole. He pounced and brought the white-fronted creature from its tiny lair. I could feel him smiling in victory.

"But I do not plan to return, Mistress, I would lose him forever." My voice choked with emotion.

"It will not be forever, Sab-ra. Your destiny is linked to Maidenstone house."

"Then why must I leave?" I wailed. "I don't understand, and I want to be here with you."

"Life turns in a wheel, Child. Sometimes one must travel what seems to be the wrong direction, to find the right destiny."

I took a deep breath. No matter where I was going, Cloudheart would be safe at Maidenstone. His safety was more important than my need for him.

"Then I will leave him," I could not say another word.

Honus walked forward. She was Cloudheart's favorite cook. She bent and picked him up. He licked her chin. I could not watch any longer. I turned to lead Yellowmane down the back path with Ghang clattering behind me. We trekked through descending terraces of budding flowers, beyond the back gate and around the city to the Wool Road. The mist rose. Crying so hard I could hardly see, I bade farewell to Maidenstone.


Does Sab-ra save the Skygrass valley? Does she succeed in her mission? Does she meet the Kosi King? Does she find an honorable justice for Hodi?

Read "The Songs of Skygrass" coming soon

*Acknowledgements*

*I am grateful to the following people who encouraged me:*

*To Theresa Crumpton, my editor and writing teacher who taught me the three questions to ask myself about each scene*

*To my daughter Lisa Fitzsimmons who is a better editor than I will ever be*

*To Maeve Pascoe who read several versions and did the cover art*

*To my friend Jo Grandstaff who thought I had enough for a complete book in the first three chapters and helped decide to make the books a trilogy*

*To my sister, Kelly, who told me to keep my own voice*

*To the MSU Community Club Writing Group ( especially my Aunt Clarice, Cele, Joanne, Kate, Kathy, Laina & Adria who is still missed), and*

*To many of my granddaughter Cassidy Hoffman's friends and fellow students at Williamston Middle School who patiently listened to me read chapters of the book aloud*